I0749793

Life, Death, and Transmutation
A Charity Anthology of Dark Poetry and Fiction

Life, Death, and Transmutation

A Charity Anthology of Dark Nature Poetry and Fiction

Edited by Alison Armstrong

Dark Moon Rising Publications | Virginia

70 Foxwood Drive
Rocky Mount, Virginia 24151
Tel: (540) 257-2861

ISBN: 978-1-945987-98-4

10 9 8 7 6 5 4 3 2 1

Printed in the United States of America

Table of Contents

Introduction to Life, Death, and Transmutation

by Alison Armstrong

"We need another and a wiser and perhaps a more mystical concept of animals. Remote from universal nature and living by complicated artifice, man in civilization surveys the creature through the glass of his knowledge and sees thereby a feather magnified and the whole image in distortion. We patronize them for their incompleteness, for their tragic fate for having taken form so far below ourselves. And therein do we err. For the animal shall not be measured by man. In a world older and more complete than ours, they move finished and complete, gifted with the extension of the senses we have lost or never attained, living by voices we shall never hear. They are not brethren, they are not underlings: they are other nations, caught with ourselves in the net of life and time, fellow prisoners of the splendour and travail of the earth."

— **Henry Beston,*The Outermost House: A Year of Life On The Great Beach of Cape Cod***

Ever since I was a child, I have often wished I could be an animal instead of a person. I wondered what it would feel like to be free of the abstract restrictions insulating humans from a more primal, sensory experience of the world. Imprisoned by linguistic, philosophical, religious, and other paradigms, we as people tend to set ourselves apart from Nature, believing ourselves superior, and, in the process, destroying forms of life much more ancient, much more interconnected with the eternal rhythms of life, death, and transmutation affecting every living being.

We create artificial worlds in an attempt to distance ourselves from our inevitable mortality, yet, despite our simulations, our ultimate fate is the same as all other earthly species. The reality of our interconnectedness is poignantly revealed in many great works of literature, such as the writings of Wendell Barry, Mary Oliver, Barry Lopez, Rainer Maria Rilke, Robinson Jeffers, and Philip K. Dick.

In *The Exegesis of Philip K. Dick*, for example, the science fiction writer's philosophical and metaphysical speculations regarding existence and the nature of reality, Dick writes, "There is nothing we know that the creatures don't know; they are our equals," sharing the same fate. "Every fly with a missing leg, every cat beleaguered by fleas, every human being fearing economic want--the endless wheel turns for all of us."

Recognizing this "endless wheel" of transmutational communion between all living beings is especially important now that we are in the midst of a climate crisis. Although the awareness of our interconnectedness may evoke feelings of fear, dread and sadness, it also helps awaken us to empathy and a deeper appreciation for our beautiful, life-sustaining planet.

A Skull and Two Digits

by Basile Lebret

Black. At first the whole world was black. And the master's fingers fed me.

This was the time of the fluff, the young feathers, the soft and yellow beak. I was a chick back then. The master's fingers were callous and smelled of dirt, of earth and the faint scent of blood. He fed me wolf bones, wolf meat; forced me to sleep within wolf hides so that I'd be used to the enemy's scent.

The meat was cold, and damp and always wet. And in the first month, the master had to tear and chew it with his teeth 'til I could be fed. I didn't know the master's teeth back then. Only the callous nature of the fingers and the harsh, harsh taste of wolves' flesh.

The world was black back then.

I remember when the master first took me outside. The world was black but the world felt large somehow. I felt wind for the first time, and the rush of it, its howling sound gave me goosebumps. The master's hands patted my head while he spoke calmly in his own language. In a tongue, I could not understand.

When the master first took off the bag, I discovered the world wasn't black. The world was wide and blue and green. It reached in all directions so far, I felt dizzy. I was standing on the master's arm and I could see his teeth, his eyes, his brownish skin.

I read in his eyes the master wanted something out of me. For the first time, I spread my wings, to their full extent. High above, the sun was a white hue that burnt my scalp. But I didn't know it was the sun. I squinted. The master spoke. And I flew.

The master took me out a few times after this. He would change the scent of the world, take off my hat, speak a single word and I was allowed to fly. When I decided to come back, either out of being tired or out of fear, I would grab his extended arm in-between my claws. The master would put the bag back on my head.

And the world would be black.

The master then taught me to hunt. First it was foxes, small red mammals and then deer and mountain goats. In due time I'd hunt wolves. As I survived each battle, I could perceive how proud the master was. We would go outside, very early in the morning. He would take off the bag, show me the target. I'd spread my wings and kill.

With each excursion, through each hunt, with each death, I saw the time inscribed itself in the corner of the master's eyes. 'Til one day, he was no more.

The fingers that fed me through this time were so small, they had to have been children's. They fed me damp food which smelled of salt. I didn't like eating this. I began to starve.

One day, the arm that carried me outside wasn't the master's arm, for the master had disappeared so long ago, I could not remember. I felt weak. The man took off the bag. He didn't speak. He didn't whisper. His eyes said nothing. I flew off.

From this day on, the world was not black anymore.

I found a mate and we mated. I learned that the sun disappears over the horizon and stars appear onto the sky and there is nothing to be afraid of. I learned that life isn't about flying to exhaustion, but a succession of small flights, of respite. Be it on a wood log, on a stone.

Have you ever witnessed the sun coming above the mountains? Have you ever taken the time to breathe in the snow when it falls? And the touch of cold that is the morning dew?

My mate bore children. And we fed them. We fed them with blood, warm flesh and egg; taken from animals I'd learned to kill the master's way. I sensed my mate's fear every time I dared attack a wolf, a deer. Creatures bigger than us. Stronger than birds of prey.

I've seen men climb up mountains to steal eggs. The master's way. I know for those chicks the world is black. And that it'd become colorful only when their beaks got hard. I wish strength upon them. I wish them good luck in their hunts.

But then the food grew scarcer. I saw the green fields crushed beneath the crude cement. I've seen the gray take hold of the earth, and now the horizon lay hidden behind a roofed curtain.

This is not the master's way.

The machines, with their noise, and their scent chased off the prey and I saw first my children, then my mate fly away in the sunset. Yet I stayed.

I stayed where I first saw the sun rise and where I first saw the sun lay. I stayed where once stood the master's abode which I never saw, which I only knew by scent.

And as the food disappeared, and I could not fight the wolves anymore. Nor the ox, nor the elk. For I grew old, weary and alone. I thought of the tiny creatures the humans bear. The fragility which lay in them.

Now before the world turns black, I hunt through gardens. I search for tiny children; I go for the eyes.

I hunt the master's way.

A Spell Of Seahorses

by Sacha Rosel

1 DAWN: MEETING

Is that your spiny form
glittering beyond corals?

Transparent wink
quivering in the chiaroscuro breath of
early phosphorescent light,
at times you swirl then vanish,
an intermittent coil of recognition
piercing through my eager eyes.

Because we've found each other.

Where spying predators cannot reach
and all the light is sucked in
by seaweeds' hypnotizing lull,
this is where our curves meet.

Sheltered
from greed, hunger and destruction
this impossible tale of ring upon ring
can now begin.

2 MORNING: DANCING

Facing one another
we bounce and bound
feeling our way along the coral tendrils
to meet each other's snouts
and toothless mouths,
joined in sublunar longing.

Here comes the lightning hook of dancing
spiralling from our tails
into each bony plate:
silvery swimming, touching -
that's the entangling synchronicity,
the feverish galloping of
one upon the other
stretching through time.

Equine, aquatic,
our movements plait and interlace
a fugue of scintillating, successive
iridescent breaths,
harrows made of colour
condensing all over your female body
mirroring mine, masculine,
orange into blue into yellow
electric pentagrams,
all-moving eyes and vertebrae
a chain of chromatic sparks flashing
through water like mist
as we descend into desire.

3 DUSK: MATING

A whole morning of floating dance has passed
between us,
dusk oozing from the edge
of the ocean
as frantically you rise
and turn into compass,
pointed to the invisible sky.
So I press against you
my bones ringed with ecstasy
framed into yours,
drifting upward as we lift our heads
and curve our backs
to become one
the other.

I feel my tail scissoring open,
a crystal cup forming along its curly line as if
by magic,
cavity taking possession of
me as I brush
against your belly.
And from its star-laden circle
a breach suddenly gapes
then culminates into
a glorious calyx
sliding inside of me,
splashing the eggs you carry
with my sap,
bubbling within my swimming tail again
magically multiplying

my singular masculine shape into
more shapes -
pollinating the prism of existence
with my inner sun.

4 NIGHT: BIRTHING

The gaseous halo of the moon spills
through the ocean
and holds my body still
as you depart into the deep night.
Chained by this rioting lives
ready to burst open,
male and motherly all into one
I wait,
feeling all grains of energy ebb
into blurred loops.
These nervous frames I now carry inside,
so thin and frail
like filigree explosions:
here comes the *qi*
emerging from the deep-sinking darkness,
condensing into forms
glowing above me,
colour quickly fading from my spine
as marine air is filled
with nourishing sounds.
Then it's an endless gold of
possibilities unchained,
singing from my loins into
these new-born bones:

unfurling into gaping ripeness
I stand erect,
and shiny little shapes come
waltzing into view,
wide open to the infalling
milkiness of dark,
sparkling like a thousand
moon-scaled dots,
spangling like musical pearls.

A ghost of liquid stars
spilled from my entrails
sing in the moving breath of
liquid darkness.
Translucent mouths humming,
they rain down like
tiny yellow hands from
my wide belly,
no longer chained to
emptiness but
free to glow upwards.
A thousand die
while all the rest survive -
soft dead stars
falling into the refulgent never,
rover of carcasses this ocean proves to be
as I faint
into the gloaming trail of birth.

5 AFTER TIME: SIMMERING

Fast fluttered then dissolved
this reversed tale
where female pollinates
and male gives birth -
a stranger, richer kind of harmony
you humans living up above
would never come to believe.

Emulsifying with water
I live and prosper,
far from the monstrous arrogance of your confined mind
measuring everything as if you were
the only ones worth celebrating
in poems as in life.

Strangled by wanton blindness
the human eye will never blink to change
nor bow to empathy
but pillage and destroy.
Efface what you don't comprehend
as if it was never there -
a luminous nowhere passing you by,
lost in the imaginary ink of dreams
you'll never see,
transfixed into our own fear
of change and transmutation,
your tongue an infestation of looking glasses
held close to your face and outward
to capture monstrosity where there is none,
while carefully hiding your own.

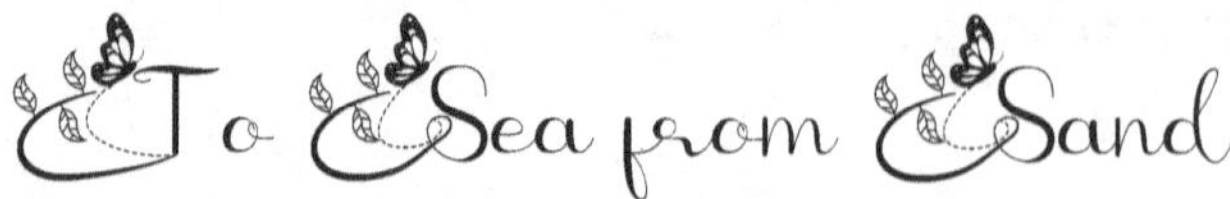

To Sea from Sand

by Juleigh Howard-Hobson

Within the waves that curl across themselves,
unfurling white
with froth on green-blue tubes, are creatures. Shell
decked, shiny bright;
people don't believe in them, so people
never see them, but
whether humans acknowledge them at all
they are still out
there. Beware of moonlit swims and evening
strolls on beaches,
don't stop and listen when the mermaids sing--
their swift reaches
exceed your ability to run and
they'll catch you, and drag you to sea from sand.

There Are Things to Avoid in the Ocean

by Juleigh Howard-Hobson

Don't tell yourself it's all a pleasant game,
the merfolk aren't here to play.
They are things
that have entrancing powers. They
don't play; they hunt. And it's always the same:
they are things
that will smile, splash, laugh, take both your hands and
pull you in. They're not boys, they're not girls,
they are things
that are bad, things with smiles, shells, pearls,
fins, tails. You are prey. You are human.
They are things.

by Juleigh Howard-Hobson

You know that it's there, watching you, and dead.
Not
a ghost, no. It's brought undefined dread,
and what
might be called a sense of utter
terror. It
feels more like a predator
than a spirit.
Ghosts are always bound
to certain places,
This has come around
from somewhere else. Spaces
that used to feel
comfortable and well-lit are
suddenly
excruciating and reveal
too much
to whatever's there. You can almost
touch
it. You know it's bad. And dead. And so close.

(reprint)
glosa

by Juleigh Howard-Hobson

(reprint, first appeared in *Memento Mori Ink* Issue 7)

There is magic in decay.
A dance to be done
For the rotting, the maggot strewn
Piles of flesh which pile---------- Dan Chelotti, "Compost"

we maggots we move we wriggle we creep
from the eggs where we once lived to beneath
the skin inside the wounds along the cuts
brothers and sisters working together
no one goes hungry we all eat we all
grow we don't ever want to grow away
here we are happy here we are what we
want to remain as we want to live
deep down inside the guts we want to stay
as we are there is magic in decay

there is softly rotting flesh and there is
warm fetid darkness tinged red and brown and
black we are pale eaters of what must be
eaten we worm our way against the spine
into lung into liver up the nose

behind the eyes we eat the mouth the tongue
the gum away from the tooth away from
the jaw we are white faces inside the
face eating the face once death has begun
to rot to stink. It's a dance to be done

we maggots we have no legs but we dance
all the same in the corrupted space that
is lifeless flesh look how we dance, we move,
we shift ourselves eating eating growing
growing longer wider how we love what
we are a plump peristaltic platoon
siblings cousins our eggs were laid among
ourselves hatching in the warmest places
first, then all over by the afternoon,
eating. For the rotting, the maggot strewn,

the greedy bodies in the fetid flesh,
the mouths open wide, for these we thank the
universe the gods the luck we share in
ripe bites and muscular motion. For we
know no other life, no other way while
we writhe and wriggle through the meat that gives
us meaning gives us ourselves, we maggots we
don't want to become things more versatile
than worms which worm in piles of flesh which pile

(reprint)

by Juleigh Howard-Hobson

(reprint, first appeared in Under Her Skin (Black Spot Books, 2022)

Rigor mortis sets in, then breaks down. Lack
of oxygen and sustenance causes
cells to stop renewing. Gut flora start
out of control proliferation, slack
spaces fill up with pressurized gases
and my corpse will burp, and my corpse will fart

before I bloat. In lieu of oxygen,
sulphur will mix with my hemoglobin

giving my body some nasty greenish
black spots. Swelling continues and my eyes
pop out of their sockets, rotten liquids
and putrefied organs begin to flush
out of my openings. A stench will rise
attracting attentions of the insects

who arrive to lay eggs. Bottle flies will
come first. Coffin flies, flesh eating beetles,

their maggots, then worms, then the birds, come to
gnaw / peck / chew / my meat, my skin, my gut
that still remains, even my hair becomes
a meal. Exposed bones will be used to chew
on, for sharpening front teeth of the rat
who ate my lungs, the mouse who sampled some

of my facial tissue. What's left will lay
in place while who I was erodes away.

(reprint)

by Juleigh Howard-Hobson

Birds freeze to death in winter woods like these
where trees snap under burdens made of snow
and air itself is frozen. Does it please
your vicious and/ or angry gods to go
ahead with sudden blizzards that blindside
everything so nothing is prepared? Or
is it merely natural that these birds died,
heads tucked beneath ice coated wings in hope
of somehow staying warm enough to live?
What a waste of feathers, and of trees. We
all die and earth remains impassive
regarding what Fate may or may not be.
Still, I hate things that such a world allows:
birds laying frozen under broken boughs.

first appeared in *Epizootics* Issue 3 2019

The Outside

by Kyle Heger

Everett enjoyed his safe, comfortable little world, where he had plenty to eat and drink, soft and warm places to sleep, a number of recreational opportunities and a lot of affectionate attention from his caretakers.

Certainly, he enjoyed looking at what lay beyond this world through windows, watching animals move in and out of the yard, some flying, some creeping, some slithering on their bellies. When the windows were opened a bit, he would even press his nose against the screen, enjoying the many scents that carried strange and stimulating messages, tilting his head to better hear the noises made by birds, by dogs, by members of his own species.

But Everett never tried to escape. He knew better than that. Because among the other scents and sights and sounds he experienced, some indicated the presence of terrible things outside, things that would like nothing better than rending him limb from limb and devouring him, things that would roll over and crush him as if he didn't even exist, things that would strike him down with blasts of fire and thunder.

One time, when he felt the screen giving way beneath his eager weight, he jumped off the windowsill back into the safety of the building's interior so he wouldn't fall out and end up … outside.

When Everett's caretakers returned home from their mysterious errands, he would greet them at the door, eager for their company but always making sure they hadn't brought with them something dangerous from the troubling outer world, something hiding behind their backs or up their sleeves.

And he was always careful not to get caught on the wrong side of the door when it was closed.

The few times he had been brought out of his home, it had been very much against his will. He'd fought and complained and tried to get away when he saw his caretakers dragging out the carrying case which, even though they'd washed it, still smelled of urine, vomit and fear. They always were able to eventually catch him, stuff him in there and lock the door on him. Then, they'd carry him outside in the case.

The feeling of being suspended in midair, swinging several feet off the ground in this horrid-smelling little prison made Everett cry out in panic and fury. His caretakers couldn't understand his language well, but they could tell he was upset. However, they assumed that they knew better than he did what was good for him. So, they smiled and cooed at him, poking their fingers into his cage, trying to comfort or distract him, but refusing to simply return him to his home immediately.

They always put him in a terrible little room that went shooting out across the world alongside a crowd of somewhat similar little rooms, all making loud noises and belching noxious fumes. His cage bumped and jumped about inside this room as it stopped and started, slowed and sped up. This was when he usually vomited from motion sickness and often couldn't stop himself from urinating out of sheer fear.

Then, they'd carry Everett out of the little room back through the open air into another building, which was the worst part of all. It was full of creatures in similar containers or tied up with lines around their necks and chests. The air was crazy with the scents and sounds of fear, rage, pain, disease and injury. Voices spoke back and forth. Doors opened and closed. Telephones rang. Buzzers buzzed.

And still there was worse to come. He would next be taken

to a room with no windows and the worst scents of all, scents that burned his nostrils. His caretakers would put him upon a slippery, shiny table. Strangers would speak to him in high voices, smile at him, feel his ribs and abdomen, wrinkle back his lips, shine a light into his eyes and ears, stick a thermometer up his rectum and poke him with needles. His caretakers let these others do these things to him without taking any action to help him other than maybe touching him with a steadying hand. Even worse, sometimes the strangers took him away from his caretakers and did these things to him.

Then, Everett would be returned to his cage, put back in the little room, taken home and allowed to escape and go hide in some safe spot until he'd recovered.

This sequence of events would usually happen only once or twice a year. And, though they were the most upsetting parts of his life, he was able, each time, to take some dim comfort in the idea that the ordeal wouldn't last long and that he'd soon return home.

Until the day came when Everett's caretakers failed to completely latch his container. As they were carrying him to the little room that moved, he bumped against the container door, and his weight made it swing open. He half fell, half jumped out, and as his feet struck the pavement, he ran as fast as he could, away from the cage, away from the little room, away from his caretakers, his one thought being to avoid going to that dreaded building.

His caretakers gave chase, two of them. Several times they almost had their hands on him, but each time he squirmed away. At last, he outdistanced them and hid behind a potted plant in a neighbor's yard. As they passed him by, chattering excitedly to each other, calling his name, he sank lower, barely daring to breathe.

Soon, they passed around a corner and Everett could no

longer see them.

His first thought was to make it back to his home, back to the place that had always meant safety. But he suddenly realized he didn't know how to get there. In his wild flight from his caretakers, he'd wound up in a place he didn't recognize.

But he knew he must try to somehow find his home. He could feel it tugging at him, urging him to return, offering him comfort and ease and welcome and familiarity. He arose and began walking away from the shelter of the potted plant in one direction, all his senses on alert, searching for some sign he was getting closer to home. If he didn't get any such sign soon, he thought, he'd go off in a different direction and keep trying until he succeeded.

Just then a shadow fell over him, a shadow from something large, towering above him. He knew he should just run without taking time to look back, but he froze. Unable to resist the temptation, he turned his head and looked up into a pair of rolling red eyes and a mouthful of sharp yellow teeth. A large hairy paw descended on him and plucked him off the ground as his legs finally began moving. A deep voice chuckled greedily and said, "My favorite: a human. Down the hatch."

Within two swallows, Everett had left the outside.

Maize 2

Perseids over an electrical field

by Irena Barbara Nagler

Dry cornstalks, a forest of portals and bones
and unseen silver flashes
susurrant, shimmering darks
where a long breath surges, a memory
of the time of flowering fields.

Scrape and whisper, husks and leaves
this field of ghosts and upright spines
receives the plunge of August stars.

a field rife with gifts like tassels to be plucked
by children wandering into dream
thrusting hands into pockets of constellations.

This crowd of sybilant stalks
is a seawall. Behind it dark waves rise
as we strain star-searching eyes.

Shadowed Love

by Irena Barbara Nagler

Little fox in shadow-wood
Finding secret long-abandoned trails

Where does the shadowed love go
to escape the great light that presses down?

Do you find your way to the desert
to seek its hidden springs
the bones at the source rich in marrow?

Do you pivot to northeast
on the magnet in your bones
and pounce on a prayer for rain
mating-howl twisting on the wind
following a smoky thread?

Will you sleep then for years
repairing all the earth
from your den of dreams?

Mushrooms

by David L Tamarin

I Introduction

I think I was eight when it happened. For several weeks my arm had grown red and swollen, itchy, flaky, and painful. I was embarrassed, and I hid it from others. It was winter so my long sleeves shielded my arm at school. At some point the painful irritating itching became too much and I grabbed one of my father's surgical knives and cut the arm open. Blackish blood shot out, blood that was filled with buzzing itchy flies. I moaned and started to feel dizzy. What I saw when I looked into my arm made me lose consciousness.

I recovered a few weeks later in a hospital bed. I don't know remember it too well, but there were great bug pulsing throbbing tumors covered in acne growing inside my arm. Through the haze of unconsciousness I heard the doctors discussing "eggs from some unknown source" and "mushroom-like growths."

When I hit puberty, acne set in and I had to start seeing a psychologist. I was terrified of things growing inside me, under my skin. I pictured my body full of hostile and alien life forms, all trying to escape from beneath the surface. And when clusters of acne sprouted out of my face I scoured them off with cleaning materials from the closet. Sometimes I poured glue over the wound so nothing would grow back. My face was a mess for years, and I was haunted, torn apart by fear and anxiety and nausea.

II Dead Cat

It all started with the cat. Torpedo.

That thing never liked me, and I had never hidden my displeasure from him.

We had adopted Torpedo at eight weeks old from the local animal shelter my fifteen-year-old daughter Veronica volunteers at on Sundays. At six years old, Torpedo had shown no signs of illness. It was actually my daughter who found him dead in the kitchen.

Jennifer and I were in the bedroom when we heard Veronica start crying hysterically. Everyone else loved the cat, our only pet. From the tone of her sobs we knew something serious was happening and we ran from the bedroom into the kitchen, where we found our daughter on the floor, lying over the remains of our blatantly dead cat. Black flies slowly circled them.

He had a strange pained look on his face and his tongue was sticking out of his mouth, flat and dry. His eyes were open but were full of some type of dust or crumbs making the orbs invisible. There was a fungus that was growing over him, and he was covered in tiny black hissing buzzing black bugs that could barely be seen.

The fungus had partially attached the cat to the floor. My wife had her hands over her mouth, in shock.

"We've got to bury him," I said as I started to lift him up when RIP he tore into pieces, part of him still stuck to the floor, the rest of him in my hand. I was shocked by how easily he tore open, and by the lack of blood to come out. "No!" screamed my daughter. There was no blood inside, just desiccated organs and more black flies. I stumbled over, off balance, and crashed to the floor. With extreme distaste and to the sounds of shouting voices I lifted the rest of the cat from the floor.

Only when we moved the cat did I see what was underneath.

Some type of small growth on the kitchen floor.

Later on we had a funeral and my wife and daughter cried as we buried the pieces of the cat in the backyard where my wife kept her garden.

When I checked back hours later, my mood somber, the small growth on the floor was still there. I looked closely yet could not identify what the strange thing was. I borrowed a microscope from our son's room (he was in college now) and picked up the growth with a knife. Under the microscope, I could see little mushrooms growing. I felt them staring back and almost dropped the microscope. My mouth dropped open in shock. I looked around quickly. You can't be the father of a household and have the others in the house see you in abject terror. I was alone. I shoved the microscope aside and I hurried upstairs to take a scalding hot shower, trying to clean what could never be cleaned.

I could still hear Veronica sobbing. I had never liked the little fucker and I ignored my daughter's cries. I felt bad, but not too bad. Torpedo had had accidents in the house, pissing outside the kitty litter box. Now the problem was gone. Still, I felt sorrow hearing Veronica cry. I knew she would get over him though. The question is, would I get over all this? All these phobias, creeping to the surface. I wanted to cut myself up until I was dead. I hated my body and what grew in it and what it caused to grow in others. I was haunted, a monster. I started fantasizing about death, about something better than this world.

That night my wife and I had unenthusiastic sex and then I pretended to fall asleep.

III Mushrooms

A few days later I returned home to work to find my wife sitting on our front porch, looking vaguely freaked out. She had been gardening in the backyard, and she had some gardening tools by her side and in her hands. She cried out and immediately ran over to me.

"Dereck, there's something I need to show you!"

I became immediately nervous, anxious.

"What is it, honey?"

"Before I show you, I have to let you know that this is going to freak you out a little bit because it's one of your phobias."

I took a step back, not wanting to hear anything more. I turned, looked at my car and briefly thought of getting back in and driving off, then forced myself to relax. I told myself to act like a man in front of my wife.

"What phobia?"

"You know... There's been some unusual growth in the backyard, and it's freaking me out. Do I call poison control? An exterminator? What do I do?"

I asked my wife where our daughter was, and she replied that she was at her boyfriend's house. His family had three cats and she was probably crying her eyes out and playing with them.

She said nothing else but turned and walked towards the back of the house. I cursed, then followed behind, wondering what the hell she had found that might freak me out so bad. I had ideas, plenty of bad ideas of what I might find.

We entered the back yard.

"They weren't here yesterday. I've been working on the back garden daily for the past couple of weeks so trust me I know. I can tell when there's a change. And these things grew overnight, last night."

What she showed me were white nebulous mushrooms covered in tiny black bugs that made a horrible sound that pierced the center of my brain. The mushrooms looked like misshapen deformed faces, some embryonic, some old and skeletal. I quickly turned my head and took a couple of steps back. I was going to be sick. As I looked away from them, the sound mercifully faded, but when I looked back at them the sound of white noise screaming filled my ears. Mushrooms, horrible evil mushrooms, always growing where they shouldn't be. They had attacked my life and now were surrounding my home. They had encroached on my territory.

Not mushrooms.

Fuck no.

And the little black bugs that were growing in the cat and flying around its carcass - they were everywhere, repeatedly trying to fly into my eyes, ears, and nose.

Then I felt a burning sensation in my arm and stopped paying attention to everything around me. There was a large boil growing on my forearm and with a scream I tore it off, only to see a mushroom spout out, all gooey and wet and bloody. Blood ran down my arms.

In a blind rage I ran at the row of mushrooms sprouting out of the lawn and threatening to overtake our house. I stomped on one, pounding it with my foot, and immediately regretted my action. The mushroom reacted as if it were a little person. Intestine-like bloody ropes shot out of the thing as a stream of tiny black bugs flew out, buzzing in the air, making their way quickly towards me. I ran, screaming, into the house. I could hear the mushrooms mourn behind me. The bugs gave chase and were faster than me, and I felt them fly into my mouth and body.

Immediately after I entered the house I threw my clothes off and took another scalding hot shower, from which I suffered severe burns. As I emerged from the shower my wife chased after me, asking what was going on. She was scared and confused and upset. I could feel the little bugs crawling around my belly, which began to bloat. It was all red from the burning water, and it stretched, threatening to explode.

They were inside me now, and I knew it. There was no hope for me. I took a pair of scissors, shut myself in the bathroom and started cutting open my leg, scooping the mushrooms and the fungi out and stomping them on the floor. Soon the place was a bloody mess. I became nauseous and left the room, having trouble walking with one leg so damaged. Jolts of pain shot through my body and exploded out the holes in my leg as I stumbled into the bedroom.

When I entered the living room I at first thought I was hallucinating. There was a giant mushroom growing on the floor that was wearing my wife's clothes. This had to be a joke. This couldn't be real. Then the phone started ringing, and I knew it was bad news about my daughter so I didn't answer. It just kept ringing and ringing.

IV The Transformation

Then I felt my legs fuse and merge together like burning steel, the skin melting and reforming so that I had just one long stump instead of two legs. My penis and balls dropped to floor and landed with an unpleasant splat. There was no blood as I sloughed off my melting skin. I watched my poor genitals quiver in a pile and burst into flames. I instinctively screamed - or tried to scream - shocked at the sight of my destroyed sex organs, but my lungs were not working and no sound came out. I was no longer breathing through my lungs, but through my skin. My arms atrophied into nothing with such speed you could watch them shrivel up. I couldn't see anything, blinded by the fungus growing out of my eyeballs.

I realized now this all came from me. I must have killed the cat. And my wife. Probably my daughter. And I was next.

My wife's transformation was on the outside only. Even though she couldn't move I knew she was alive, trapped, perhaps for eternity. It was then that I knew what fate held in store for me. Inwardly, she was aware of it and terrified. I was frozen, staring at her, not understanding what I was seeing. Her body started moving in convulsions and there seemed to be a giant substance like mashed potatoes leaking out of her. It was as if she was foaming out the mouth, except the foam came out of her entire body and made a pool on the floor. But my mind was blown and I was terrified and not seeing and thinking clearly, and I passed out, but remained frozen in place. My wife looked as strange to me now as she did before the change. Maybe I had never been human.

My hair fell out in clumps and my head expanded. I gagged in agony as my skin tore, and my lips were pulled to their furthest before they split open, splurting out a thick viscous black fluid that dripped down my body.

My mind slowed down to a snail's pace. I stopped thinking. I knew I was dying, or maybe something worse, transforming, becoming a giant infected bug-covered fungus.

My only thoughts were on how to spread the disease further, infect more people, transform more people into creatures like me. But the voices in my head reassured me that this was happening everywhere, all across the world, and there wasn't anything to do but wait until we had control of the planet. I would have grinned if I could. Instead, tears spilled from where my eyes used to be and I toppled over, choking and gagging. I watched as a small army of mushroom men walked into the room and began tying me up. I tried to scream but I couldn't. I tried not to see but I could. What were they going to do with me? Where were they taking me? I tried as hard as I could to shut my mind down, and it worked.

Blackness descended over everything as I said goodbye to the world I once I knew.

V One Mind

Then I could see again. I could see everywhere. We mushrooms were all united in one mind, and there was a great powerful humming sound that gave me power. Tonight they'll bury me, and I'll rise from the ground an even stronger mushroom, ready to destroy your world. You'll never stop us.

Ever.

We, The Wildflowers

by J. L. Lane

As wildflowers rise from the dark, sodden earth,
So too do we awaken at our hour of birth.
Fragile and tender, with roots still so small,
The morning of life holds promise for all.

In youth we flourish, like midsummer's light,
Chasing horizons, unbridled, eyes bright.
The fields are alive with light and laughter,
Believing the daylight will linger long after.

But autumn brings with it a much gentler grace,
Lines drawing the years—wisdom on the face.
Colours of memory darken and dye,
While time reminds us the years rush by.

Then winter drifts on with a silvery breath,
Slowing soft steps to the valley of death.
Barren the branches, their blossoms long gone,
They wither in silence, as the dark lingers on.
Every blossoming flower, eventually will wilt,
Time will crumble everything that was built.

Once winter fades, and gives way to the spring,
New life will bloom, and fresh choirs will sing.
The withered and fallen, returned to the ground,
Their silence the cradle where new life is found.

In death they surrender what once they possessed,
To nourish the earth for the lives yet to rest.
The death of the old is the soil for the new,
A cycle unbroken, eternal, and true.

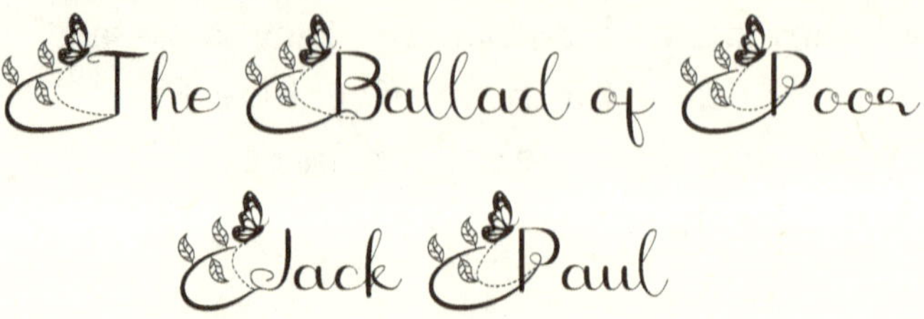

The Ballad of Poor Jack Paul

by J. L. Lane

'Twas in the early hours,
During the very first breath of spring,
Amongst the newly blossomed flowers,
Just as the birds began to sing.

That is where the baby was born,
So fragile and so small,
Drinking the dew of the early morn,
He was given the name, Jack Paul.

A sprite so tiny and delicate,
Wrapped within a flower's hold,
The morning sun did soon beget,
A glow of living gold.

The robins came to watch and sit,
And sing the day awake nearby,
The breeze did stir, the flowers lit,
Beneath the warming sky.

By the time the summer came,
Jack was now a lad,
Who ran around and played his game,
Of Hop on the Lily Pad.

He danced amongst the pollen,
And skipped upon the rain.
The fields of summer called to him,
Through meadow, hill, and lane.

But time is all too short you see,
And summer had to end.
It had been filled with fun and glee,
But now Fall crept round the bend.

Now grown into a fair young man,
His step was firm, his voice was strong,
He walked the fields where once he ran,
And hummed a fleeting song.

Autumn brought the balding trees,
How sad that they did look,
And in the chill of the changing breeze,
Jack would soon be out of luck.

He ventured forth one late–autumn night,
To chase the winds astray,
But found their strength a sudden might,
Which carried him away.

It blew him down the hill so fast,
Into the valleys dark,
He landed with an awful crash,
Into a pile of bark.

Poor Jack lay still in the cold,
For moments lost, or ages long,
His fate was never to grow old,

As winter wove its chilling song.

You see, as Jack had tumbled down,
From atop that steep hill,
He had, alas, broken his crown,
And remained there in the chill.

The ice did come to bury Jack,
Where he did rest so still,
Yet Jack in time would surely be back,
And with him, he would bring the chill.

Jack now drifts through mortal lands,
To wander where the cold winds cross,
His shadow trailing icy hands,
A spirit born of frost and loss.

Each winter Jack does come to call,
To dance amongst his icy gloss,
No longer is he called Jack Paul,
Now all know him as… Jack Frost.

by Mawr Gorshin

I am Drofurb, Crim of the soil, rock, and plants of the Earth. Every grain of sand, every speck of dirt, every pebble, and every seed is an atom in my vast, brown, round body.

My three brothers are the Crims of the other elements—Weleb, the air, Nevil, fire, and Priff, water. "What is a Crim?" you may ask. A word like 'god' or 'spirit' wouldn't *exactly* convey the idea, but such words can orient a human being towards an understanding, so one *could* use such words if one wished to.

We Crims connect sentient life with the ground of all being, Cao, the ocean-like waves and rhythms of everything. Another way to conceive of that ground of all being is in the Pluries, the rain-like particles within the entire universe. A physicist might call Cao and the Pluries the particle-wave duality.

We all are the reality no human eye or ear can grasp. We are also a reality no one can escape...especially after death. We don't communicate with words normally, but we shall do so on this occasion, so you can know the process of how human life leaves your sensory world and enters ours. For man must know the consequences of his wicked acts, as will Finn Lawrence, CEO of the multinational investment management corporation, BrownStone.

His funeral finally over, the guests now leave the cemetery, though they—including his surviving family—are not exactly mourning his loss, for few ever liked him; they have attended largely out of obligation. The coffin is underground. At last, there will be peace and quiet.

Except for a soon-to-come light drizzle.

Each drop of this drizzle falling on the ground where Lawrence's grave is will contain more than mere water.

Pluries, dwellers in the raindrops, are essences in the universe that the senses don't perceive…not without a thorough training that is rare among humanity.

My brother, Priff, is the spirit in the water that connects everything to Cao and the Pluries. Lawrence's body and soul will meet these three water-like essences.

During his life, Lawrence was particularly ignorant of these essences, since he was only concerned with material gain…a gain that came to him at my—Drofurb's—expense. Now, he will learn those essences, however painful that learning will be.

Yes, here comes the rainfall now, soaking the grass of the cemetery. Priff is now seeping into my soil and making contact with Lawrence's coffin.

Since Priff and I surround his body—which is the same as his soul, but on a different frequency—we two Crims will take his soul on a journey: from the crudely material world in which he lusted after wealth and power, to the oneness of Cao.

Priff oozes past the wooden cracks of the coffin, causing that wood to dissolve, little by little. Priff drenches the surrounding soil. My brother and I strengthen each other in our union.

Lawrence no longer has consciousness, of course—not waking, sense-perception—but his soul can experience the unconscious dream world, and here he will know both the heaven…and the hell…of ego death.

Ego death is heaven for those rare ones who have meditated, practiced self-denial, and have loved their fellows.

It is hell, a lengthy purgatory, for selfish, greedy people like Lawrence.

Indeed, throughout his career as he rose in the ranks to CEO of BrownStone, Lawrence eagerly agreed with the corporation's policies that resulted in the ruthless pollution of the Earth—financing wars, chopping down trees, dumping toxic waste in rivers, lakes, and oceans, and stuffing landfills all over the world.

Defiling Priff and me, in other words. BrownStone is a cancer in my brown stones.

In Lawrence's love of accumulation without thought of the harm he was doing to us, Nevil's passionate fire heated his heart, and Weleb blew Lawrence about, leaving him lost in the winds of confusion. Now, we opposing Crims, Priff and myself, Drofurb, must restore balance and bring Lawrence back the other way, to Priff's watery, cool serenity and to my earthy, firm stability.

We have now completely disintegrated the coffin, and the wet soil, a fusion of Priff and me, touches Lawrence's already decaying skin. Since body and soul are one, this intermingling of him with what's outside of him combines *atman* and *Brahman*, or his personal soul with Cao, the World-Soul, which is all wavelike energy.

The dream world of his personal unconscious becomes one with the unconscious of everything…whether he wants it, or not…and he *won't* want it.

He feels my pain, the pestilence of the fouled soil…a soil tainted and contaminated by the pollution of landfills and the ravages of war worldwide, destruction caused by the weapons manufacturers that BrownStone has invested in, with Lawrence's consent.

In his dream world, he sees himself falling into a brown, reeking pool of liquid shit. He wishes he could scream, but without a living, physical body, he has no voice. His 'spiritual body,' as it were, has splashed into the filthy brownness.

His whole body submerged, he tries to swim up to the surface, not to breathe, for lacking an actual body, he has no need to breathe. It's just the idea of being in this disgusting lake of feces that is so insufferable.

All that shit…he can smell it. Its closeness to him is unbearably offensive. And as much as he tries to swim up to the surface, he can't find it.

Without a voice, he can only think his words.

How did I get here? he wonders.

We are making you experience, in a sense, what you put us all through, I tell him in a voice that rings and echoes in his mind's ear.

Put you *all through? Put* who *all through? Who are you? The last thing my soul remembers is being put in a grave in a cemetery, a beautiful, clean, peaceful place, a place my investment company never came near, let alone polluted. How can the soil of my grave be connected with the landfills of places so far away from here?*

My ringing voice thunders in a rage at Lawrence. *The soil here is connected with the soil all over the Earth through myself, Drofurb, the Crim of the soil, earth, rock, and plants! I, Drofurb, unite all of the globe's soil, so that everywhere, we mounds of dirt, rock, and sediment feel the same pain, as if the landfills far away, on the other side of the Earth, were right here in the cemetery.*

Dirt isn't alive, Lawrence thinks. *Soil can't be alive.*

WE ARE ALL ALIVE…AND YOU MUST PAY!

It was just business, though! What I did was all just…

BUSINESS? What you did was just inundate me with filth! Hence, I'm drowning you in filth!

But what's the point of putting me through this? Lawrence asks me. *How will torturing me clean the Earth?*

We aren't doing this for the Earth, I tell him. *We're doing this for* you.

For me? *This is supposed to* help *me?*

Yes.

How?

Through this, you are going to learn how to stop cutting yourself off from the world and to reconnect with it. All your life, Lawrence, you have lived only for yourself: seeking monetary gain, chasing women, bullying and bossing around employees, rising up the echelons of power without any consideration for the people, plants, and animals you've hurt or killed. It's time you learned how to feel for every living thing outside of yourself.

And how am I supposed to do that, Mr. Soil-Ghost?

By merging with the outside world, Mr. Lawrence.

What?

Now he feels a kind of acidic liquid burning into him.

Oww! That hurts! What is it?

Acid rain, I tell him.

Acid rain? How did that get here?

From you, *Mr. Lawrence.*

What?

Yes. Don't you have any idea what BrownStone does to the world? Are you that *insensitive to your corporation's destructiveness? All the factories, power plants, and vehicles that BrownStone has invested in over the decades have released large amounts of sulphur dioxide and nitrogen oxides when burning fossil fuels. The acid rain damages man-made structures, it harms aquatic ecosystems, and it damages forests and crops.*

Lawrence has nothing to say now. All he can do is feel the burning of the acid rain as it flows through my soil and seeps into his skin.

You must feel this pain to understand, Lawrence. You must become one with the earth to understand, too.

He wants to scream as he feels the acidic liquid not only burn him, but also accelerate the dissolution of his body. He is becoming one with the soil around him, and also with the sea of shit in his dream.

Is there no escape from this hell? he wonders.

There is, I tell him, *but the only way out is* through. *You must endure this ordeal right to the end, and only then will you find peace.*

How can I endure such excruciation?

By feeling compassion.

Compassion?

Yes, I tell him. *You must* suffer with *the soil, earth, rock, and water that your investments helped harm.*

His body and soul fragment into pieces; I'm ripping them up into tiny shreds. Then I rip those shreds into tinier ones, then those into even tinier ones, over and over again.

He feels sharp pains all over. He and I are intermingling.

No, he thinks. *I want to continue being as I am.*

No, I tell him. *You mustn't continue thus. You must give up your ego.*

As the fragments of himself separate and drift apart, they continue to intermix with his surroundings, my soil. During this mixing, he starts to feel the *consciousness* of those surroundings…*our* pain.

Oh, no, he thinks as he feels it. *What have I done?*

He can feel the filth of the garbage in the far-off landfills as it contaminates my soil, for all the soil of the Earth is *one*. The filth feels like a growing infection, a sickness, a plague.

This is…nauseating, he thinks.

The acid rain burns his fragments; it eats into the tiny pieces that used to be his body and soul. If he had a voice, he'd scream in agony.

He finds himself transforming into a tree in a forest…yet he sees men with axes chopping down the trees. Though these are trees other than himself, he can feel each strike of the axes cutting into the wood, as if they were cutting off the arms and legs of his living body, for all the plants of Drofurb are one. He shudders as he sees the axemen coming closer and closer to him.

If he could only scream.

The axemen arrive. They surround him. As they hack into his wood, he feels like a victim in a slasher film. He can only stand there and take the whacks.

Next, he imagines he's a huge, wide-open mouth. Above it is a huge canister, on the side of which are the four intersecting black rings of the biohazard symbol.

Oh, God, no! he thinks. *Don't make me drink that!*

He is forced to gulp it all down. He wants to puke it out, but he can't.

A dull ache ripples through him like nausea. The toxic drink transforms him. Now, instead of a mouth, he's an ocean…a polluted one.

Filth and garbage float all about him.

I feel like an unflushed toilet, he thinks.

Finally, that filthy ocean hardens within seconds into a flat, desert area, sparsely dotted with small patches of grass. He's all dirt, like the dust Adam would return to. Far off, he can hear an airplane flying.

It's getting closer…and louder.

At first, there's a beautiful blue sky with a few clouds. Then, a huge shadow comes over him.

It's the shadow of the plane.

A bomber plane.

He wishes he could shudder, move like an earthquake, as he sees the first of several bombs dropping from the plane.

They're falling…closer and closer to him.

No, please...NO! he thinks, helpless and wishing his thoughts could be heard, wishing he could dodge the bombs.

As the bombs hit him, he feels the dirt and soil fly in all directions. It's all him, his body and soul, shattering into thousands, tens of thousands of pieces.

The fragments, as small as grains of sand, are flying so far apart as to be galaxies away from each other. Each piece is so alone, so isolated.

So tiny and insignificant.

Each is floating on an infinitely vast ocean of water now.

Each little speck feels as alone as Lawrence felt his whole life. Now he no longer just feels alienated from the world; he feels alienated from himself.

But that floating on an endless ocean is making all the specks moisten, loosen, and melt. As the water intermingles with each speck, the specks fuse with their surroundings...the soil that is *me*.

His merging with what's all around him ends his loneliness. He now knows why he chased money, power, and women his whole life.

He was trying to compensate for his loneliness, caused by a neglectful family that only pushed him to make money for them and never showed him affection.

...and while making the money, he never succeeded in filling his emotional void.

This merging with the All, though, with me and with Cao, is bringing his loneliness to an end.

He no longer fears the dissolution of his ego...he is starting to like merging with everything else. It feels like joining a community.

As he merges, though, he feels the pain of the world—the pain he caused me. Now, he no longer feels shame from it, the kind of shame that would make him want to resist the merging…no; he feels guilt, compassion, and an urge to heal all the wounds he helped cause.

He wants reparation with me.

Now, he thoroughly welcomes the merging with me.

His tiny fragmented pieces are melting all the faster, being diluted into the surrounding water of his dream and the soil of his physical reality, and they are becoming one with me. His ego is fading away.

He likes no longer being an *I*, for now, he is a *we*.

He is *me*, Drofurb of the soil and earth.

He is part of an infinite world, full of friends.

It's a peaceful, soothing, slow flow of mystical waves rippling everywhere.

He is one with Cao.

by Pixie Bruner

It was always there.
It sat behind his reading chair as he watched TV.
It sat at the empty seat at the empty nest dinner table.
It was laying out on the coffee table beside the remote.
It was in the cracks of every sidewalk
Reliable as the worn slippers at your feet. Yet, you refused it.

"Sort of worked" does not make it disappear,
set off on a one-way trip to a far off horizon you'll never see.
It was still there like the reading glasses you constantly lose.
It was still there like your aches and pains,
a constant thing, ever-present.
The page a day could not add additional pages for comfort.

It was always ready and waiting,
like that best of good dogs for its master at the end of the day.
It was ready, even if you were not, an ever best boy.
It could not nod its head at your refusal.
It could not pause and rewind for your comfort.
It would not ever go away. Loyalty unmatched. Kind animals.

You ignored the calendar,

made assumptions, made a dreamworld,
you stopped all the clocks prematurely
not realizing that time still flew without you,
not acknowledging the sand was still drifting
the ample curved hourglass increasingly bottom-heavy.

It did not catch you off-guard, come out of nowhere.
You stood there and observed it for many years.
thinking, perhaps, if I don't talk to it, it will ignore me.
Maybe if I refuse to see it, look at its empty eyes,
despite those limbs becoming twigs,
your daddy becoming as spindly as daddy long legs.

It was sitting beside you all your life.
The silent companion gnawing on every moment
The one who never abandoned you for even a minute.
Now, you finally face it head on, and after the fact,
you pretend you never knew or noticed
the rictus grin of the skull - the eternal true face beneath
all flesh.

Interlocked

by Alison Armstrong

Glazed eyes stare at him,
in head to head contact.
Antlers locked in deathly combat.
wherever he goes,
his rival's face confronts him,
matted fur bedecked with snow-white confetti,
the loser's laurels
sheltering maggots.
He, the victor,
languishes,
stench of death
smothering the scent of pine,
memento mori
mocking
with rictus sneer
his wintry starvation.
Driven by doe-lust
the two stags dueled,
rut-roused tempers clashing.
Bone to bone they scraped
their skull-crowned weapons
charging, slashing.
until one head,
detached from its body,
remained captive
to the decapitating foe.
Conjoined by ardor-driven fate,
The losing combatant

has become his fatal mate.
Will decay sever
his imprisoning bond
or will the rot spread
until both lie dead?

Lizard

by Alison Armstrong

Small as an insect,
you snuck inside the door,
seeking cool darkness.
I, too, shun the sun,
The scorching vastness,
larger yet more empty
than anything finite can imagine.
We meet inside a pantry
filled to sate
the ravenous fears.
You flee
grappling fingers,
encircling domes.
You evade
my attempted deliverance
back into
the searing light.
You flail until
you can no longer fight.
Only husk remains
of struggle,
limp surrender
drying in the sun,
as I hide
in the shadows,
aching for reprieve.

by Alison Armstrong

A sentient product
of human arrogance
and rapacious technology,
you restlessly roam
your simulated wilderness
man-cultivated like yourself,
grafted and spliced,
a safe,
stifling paradise.
Within you stirs a chaos,
a primordial pulse
defying denatured constraints.
A faint stirring of the wind
brings the scent of large, lumbering prey
wild and free
and your belly,
unsated
with pre-butchered meat
growls.
Somewhere
beyond imprisoning confines,
from within dark, sheltering pines
you hear the beckoning howls,
of your kindred,
Untamed,
unstained by Anthropocene conceits.
In Ice Age memories
you are with them,

hunting and feasting,
wild and free.

by Christina Guldi

Yeah, I used to go. I used to participate. Everyday. Twice. Every diurnal cycle. You remember?

Oh, that's right. You don't, do you?"

***

The moment the moisture on the heads of the leaves was the thickest, I could smell it. The time the dark would begin to fragment at the edge of the world, I could sense it. The crackling of insects wiggling beneath the soil, between the caverns of roots and mycelium, I could hear it. My eyelids would begin to tremble matching the tingling deep in my belly, seeping into the narrow tunnels of my feathered bones. It wasn't an urge or a calling. It was so much more. It was compulsive. There was nothing like it. This compulsion, this Surge, electrified my entire body and mind. There was no choice but to awaken and soar into the magnetized wave which directed me to my collective.

No one led, you see? No one followed. We just were. We were one being in pure harmony. A hyper focus of directionless flow. No one knew how it started each time. Our destined locations were not predetermined. We all just knew which family of trees, which set of wires. It was a sudden evaporation of self. Pure ecstasy. Trust. Knowing. Our sonic dance of intimately strangled breath blasted octaves too high for the mammals to hear. This, intertwined with the displacement of the air bouncing off fluttering wings, created a geometric symphony of swirling fractals. We transcended time and thought. Unaware of our surrendering to this Surge, everything and nothing, everyone and no one mattered. A spiraling vocal mitosis. A steadily building feedback loop of screeching tongues and chirping beaks burst into a frenzy of praise and radical love. A confetti rain of down feathers swayed themselves towards the land below, some becoming trapped in the wedges of branches in the descent.

We didn't need wings to fly anyway. Not at that moment, not then. Hurricanes of the most vibrant warbler blues and flamingo pinks pulsated between us, connecting us into a grid patterned network of radiant shimmering bliss. Caws, squawks, cries raging into the drumbeat of the dawn. This was Creating. WE WERE Creation.

The Sun's slow ascent would pierce his light through the labyrinth of concrete and foliage and skin and steel, gradually heating the surfaces of everything below. As the earth warmed, the frequency of our worshiping trance cooled. A dim alertness would leak in from all directions, making cracks in our collective consciousness, bringing with it a recognition of solidified individuality. The unified sonnet would dissolve into differentiated singular voices. Our eyesight narrowed, focused, newly sensitized to the coming day's movement. The intensity of sun rays reflected into our eyes from the roofs of vehicles and pools of water, jolting us back into our daily tasks. We dispersed, each with our own agenda. Foraging, fucking, and frolicking until near dusk when the Surge would take hold from deep within us, uniting us again into a timeless existence before the Sun sank his light into the edges of the other side of the world.

I cannot pinpoint the exact moment I began to wonder. Those first doubts, I do remember, though, came long before you pipped years ago, during a season when the land was so very dry. Many of us died searching for any nourishment among the scarcity. Yet through the grief, the Surge undeniably continued to dwell within us with the same level of vigor.

There was a change, however. Its source?...I still ponder. The not knowing troubles me so much that I still sometimes restlessly struggle when deciding on where to roost at night. There is no logical reason to feel unsafe, but when a waxing moon rises, I feel deeply unsettled. Just a hint of a threat waiting. Waiting patiently for me. To teach me a lesson of sorts. Just for me, in the lower, denser clouds just above the canopy.

As you know, the males do not require the same amount of nourishment our bodies do. In that season, food was so rare in the blanched landscape that we resorted to consuming unnatural vermin, vermin that we, nor our cloaca, knew how to easily digest. Yet, the Surge continued on with as much ferocity as ever. Several of our males had a vitality that still demanded to be satisfied. Many sisters joyously obliged to their dutiful instinct. Some mildly resisted, but quickly succumbed to social pressure. Others like me, were overpowered and taken by force. And there we were, emaciated, imprisoned by our biology and trapped in a transitional land. Some males lingered alongside the sisters, diligently harvesting the broken scraps. Most of the males carelessly went about their lives, free from any responsibility or care for those they recklessly created and abandoned. Our bulging ovaries held intact by fragile frames were strained to their deadly limits. I continued to be stirred by the Surge which blindly guided me to the gatherings every morning and each evening. A sogginess of my will started to settle in, sitting heavy, becoming more saturated with each stop along our migration; the same stops where our ancestors had gathered, sang and frenzied on their long journeys to the same destination.

Yes, daughter. We did indeed make it. Well, some of us. Many of us scarred, but together, alive. Closing in on our nesting land, we honed in on the smells of the familiar security, the relief from exhaustion. This olfactory recognition ignited a collective burst of last-ditch motivation as our open-ended-triangle accelerated through the sky. Never had I tasted such sweet anticipation as which we shared in that moment.

You know the vibrational warnings we pass along during flight? The signal I received was similar in shape and temperature as the one we use for land-bound beasts, but carried a nuanced heaviness that I did not understand or had previously felt. Reflexively mimicking the alert to my sisters behind me in mid-soar, I looked down and I saw it with my own eyes. It hit me like a windshield. If the thick breeze wouldn't have kept me in flight, I would have plummeted to my death in shock. Our ancestral grounds were now an unrecognizable catastrophic hellscape of mud and debris featuring rivets so large, we could not imagine a beast capable of creating them. Drenched in rust colored sludge, the peaks were crusted dry with smashed stems, leaves, stones, sticks poking out in every direction resembling statues perched frozen in an angry fertility dance. We didn't know what to do. So we did what we've always done. We landed and did our best. Stories of destruction from floods, volcanoes, and fires have been passed down along with stories of survival and perseverance. I know my story sounds futile, It isn't unique, you think. And it may not be.

This is not a story passed down to me though, you see? I argue that my experience is unique. Our destruction wasn't over in a day or two like a storm, no. As far as we knew, this was unprecedented. It lasted the entire season, perhaps longer, we don't know, as the magnetic pull of winter called us back to our darker homeland before we saw an end to this rampage. Giant yellow land-bound beasts moved in with roars and growls that did not cease until moonlight. They did not run or walk, but slithered like clumsy snakes that ate dozens of our unborn when they only had enough stomach for one or two. Flight was our only escape. There was no true rest. We had to build our nests, you see? I did manage to find a hollow in a tree. I strenuously pecked away and pulled the plant debris out from the crusted crests of the rivets. The Surge still ran through our blood and kept us going. It kept us together even when we had to spread out to survive. We were in close enough proximity to hear one's distant calls, but a cautious formality replaced the intimacy we used to share. No one felt truly safe. Our brief time together was the only joy, the only sense of normalcy I had left.

One morning when returning to my nesting project, I discovered my hollow overturned on its side. Twice the width and length of when I had left. Roots and all, exposed and panting. If I hadn't been so devastated, I would have found the sight a magnificent one. Still a bit tingly from the Surge, I was able to block out my despair for a few moments to seize the opportunity to fill my belly with the thousands of ants frantically salvaging their unborn with little success. The situation's irony was not lost on me.

All my progress was gone and my time was running thin. Brooding instincts make you do unimaginable things I am too ashamed to repeat to you. I was told one of our sisters had already laid all her young when she found a place she felt was safely hidden after carefully observing it for some time. Soon after, one of those yellow beasts came slithering clumsily toward her and her family. Too young for them to escape on their own, she was forced to make a decision no mother ever should. She witnessed them all swallowed in an instant. I never did see her again, but I was told she still wanders about. She has been seen often trying to defend phantom eggs she is incubating in nests which have been abandoned seasons ago, snapping at any perceived intruder. I am aware I was not the only one who managed to lay that year in a half-constructed nest held together with insecurity and hope. I was also not the only one who laid shells that were soft to the touch.

I know that look. You aren't the first to look at me that way. We live in abundance, you all say. And perhaps you are right. There are plenty of caged plastic tubes refilled regularly by the Gentles with dead seeds and dehydrated worms. Plenty of elevated warm corners to raise our young under spiked florescent lights. Newly innovated flexible insulating materials like dental floss, condom wrappers, and dryer lint is easily acquired. For you it is natural. It is all you've known. Some of the older ones even claim this as an improvement.

We made it through. We adapted. As a species. And life goes on. And the Surge continues. But at what cost? You wanted to know my story. Why I no longer join. I don't know. But I know it wasn't a choice in the true sense. I cannot comprehend how anyone can survive a season like that one and not be compelled to wonder, to ask questions, to doubt. For seasons the Surge still rhythmically aroused me out of slumber. I heard the crackling, I smelled the dew, I felt the pulsating. The wave of magnetized love I used to glide in started to require more effort each morning. There was a resistance. A friction I hadn't felt before. The frenzied trance was still beautiful and comforting, but transcendence did not flow. I struggled with this for a long time. I suppose I still do.

Did I change? Did our songs change? I yearned. Where was that loving intelligence that manifested instinctively within me? Was I broken? I felt betrayed and wounded. I still went. But the trance no longer consumed me, I was simply going through the motions. Desperately wanting was not enough. This lack forced me to question. What is Creation? Who is Creating? I used to know without a doubt that the answer was Us. But I didn't feel that with certainty any longer. What sort of creator would force us to consume one another in order to merely survive? Eating was still a necessity, but I mostly tasted guilt. And it all unraveled. I unraveled. What was once a harmonic display of timeless ecstasy just looked messy. Inauthentic. Chaotic. Silly even. No matter how I sang or how I fluttered, I was still just me. And they were...them. I felt disgust witnessing their stupidity and false faith and I hated myself for that. Who were they trying to convince? One another or themselves? Do they believe the mythology of our greatness? All the magick I trusted and took for granted was gone. Could our collective instincts have tricked us into willingly participating in cycles of causing pain and enduring suffering? I found any possible theory repulsive. I was heartbroken. I felt incomplete without Us. During the gatherings, I envied them. I pitied them. I was ashamed of them. I missed them. I still feel all of these things. I believe I will always feel the Surge, but as a hum. The purr of a paranoid cat.

I still do not know if I lost connection or I gained a knowledge which I cannot unknow.

I understand I am not alone in my doubt or detachment. An unspoken divide within our tribe was becoming apparent. From the safe distance of our individual nooks, a few of us outsiders would mock them for the obliviousness of their own demise. For their praising a creator for stale flavorless food. Do they not recall how seeds directly from the flower tasted? We laughed among ourselves. Mocked them for sharing in delirium twice a day, everyday with others who are capable of conveniently discarding them when they are the most in need? Do they not see how tattered and dull their feathers look from the treated pools of stagnant water the Gentles leave? How can they celebrate like this, when this is what we have become? We know some of them think we are being punished with sadness for our unfaithfulness. Some pity us. They cannot see that it was not a choice. We refuse to feel gratitude for a world we did not consent to. We refuse to unknow what we know. We cannot unsee the cruelty of instinct. And yet, we feel the Surge deep down inside. The purring of a paranoid cat.

***

I love you, daughter. I believe in you. Maybe I am broken. Or maybe a coward. I cannot bear to watch you being swallowed in one instant by a beast, or slowly over a short sickly lifetime. Maybe I'm trying to justify my cynicism. I don't know. I have to go now. But I do know that I love you very, very much. This is the best, but the most difficult way that I know how to love you.

Float Away

by Shawn Scott Smith

The burning of dead things continues,
Ashes rising to atmosphere, like a mother's kiss,
Up up and away, into lore, and legend.
Until the cumulus turns into nimbus,
Blood rain falls on the newly born trees,
The ancestors washing it in perpetual rhythm,
Carbon, letting out a wild yell.
The wolves hunt with abandon,
Smells of sweet victory on the mountain trail,
A lingering method to disease and pollution,
Wondering what these atoms will become next,
When I am laid in the earth,
My language gone,
A last breath to steal,
One last look at the brilliance of it all.

Adrian at Sea

by Kristi Hendricks

The poachers rode the waves
Silent and at sea
Gathering ammunition as it were
Against the ocean and immortality.
Cetaceans swam and glided through melody
Made to reverberate in the ocean in rhapsody.

Unbeknownst to the mortal villains
Who only valued life in terms of fleeting currency
Was a creature under the ancient water
With body of bulletproof scale
And teeth sharper than martyr swords.

When a pod of rorquals came into view
The modern predators with their cruel steel
Collaborated on death
To steal from the ocean
A gift to the planet
Of balance and song.

Adrian, that dragon beast, whom Gaia sometimes guided
To protect what might be lost
Before due time, and in an overbalance of greed and mechanization
Swam to the factory ship
Determination in his reptilian eyes

Where red flame resides.

Large enough to wreck several city blocks
With one blow of the long, muscled tail,
Adrian, with his black and white, orca-patterned scales
Lifted the industry ship from below with his immeasurably strong back
Confusing the whalers as their world shifted
Into an abyss of terror
Some falling down the slipway at the stern
Where baleen carcasses were hoisted
Only to slip and fall into the water, and
Be snapped up in a colossal alligator-like snout.

Adrian grinned within
Knowing the men were in shock
Fearing for their lives
As body parts fell to the ocean
To be fed upon by sharks.

The dragon lifted his glossy tail
And branded another blow into the ruthless vessel
Intent solely on profit.
The helicopter soaring high above, to aid in whale spotting
Was dispatched at will
In Adrian's equally cruel jaws
As the great beast leapt from the ocean's din
To save the wildlife, as he saw, was his kin.
Parts of the unnatural machine fell into the water.
But Adrian's dragon breath, a holy sepulcher of natural faith
Burned these up, leaving nature unmarred.

Adrian worked the ocean for months on end

Saving the precious ecosystem from the human malice
That was intent on profit at all costs
His body one with the elements
Determined to protect wildlife

Dead Fish, New Fish

by J. Rocky Colavito

The leviathan that ruled the deep dark didn't like trespassers; the puny beings in the strange wide-eye under-sea explorer had learned the hard way about that. His huge jaws had made short work of the contraption. Once crushed, the things inside oozed out like the innards, making for a jumble of flavors that coated his palate but did little to slake his appetite. His prehistoric brain dimly recalled that one of those faux-fish things usually meant that there were others, and so the huge creature with the conical head and the mouth that looked like a circular sawblade started circling in a widening gyre, looking for evidence of more interlopers.

The beast was the size of two school buses, and while it looked like a shark, there were additions from other species that roamed the deep dark. It was a hybrid form, courtesy of its father, a helicoprion, raping its mother, a juvenile Megalodon, so its length and girth were all Meg. The jaws were its father's. It had what observers—not that the beast knew this—called a headlight in the middle of its forehead, and its front flukes were tipped with sucker-laced tentacles, like those of a giant squid.

The creature knew nothing of how it came to be an unholy mishmash of different deep dark dwellers; it had existed just fine on its own after its parents rejected it. Its hunting instinct surpassed theirs because it had somehow acquired the gift of stealth, using its ability to expel a cloud of inky cover as it pursued and engaged its prey. It also was cursed with the desire for revenge, and it had waited for its chance to kill the parents that had abandoned it. His father never knew what hit him until his belly was slashed open by the serrated mouth; his innards were dragged out by the tentacles. He became easy prey for a school of his pre-adolescent brethren.

His mother had taken a little longer and had put up more of a fight. The scars on his head and dorsal fluke were still visible. But he had prevailed, using his tentacles to drag his mother ever deeper into the abyss, forcing her into a crack in an undersea mountain and leaving her to struggle until her body succumbed to the pressure. The smaller creatures who were able to withstand the deeper dark fed well that day.

The dimness of those conquests clung to him like the remoras that accompanied sharks that lived in the light, small predators accompanied by even smaller scavengers, certainly no match for the leviathan that carefully searched for some sign of the intruders.

His search bore fruit. A dimly lit product of the surface dwellers rewarded the effort. The muted lights paled in comparison to the iridescence of the small fish that scurried about in large schools, changing shape in artistic ballet in an effort to deter predators. The leviathan had no interest in their antics. He was more intrigued by the fact that the structure was again inhabited. He also had no interest in what mischief the interlopers might be about, but this presence as an invasion of his territory would be dealt with quickly and prejudicially.

He circled the thing, a collection of out reaching spheres connected to a central rectangle by tunnels where he could glimpse the little creatures moving within. His "headlight" resembled that of other dark deep creatures, so his true form had not yet been noticed. He watched patiently.

He could sense disturbance from one side of the structure, and he swam toward it from a distance. He could see a large panel in the side of the sphere open and something huge being shoved into the depths. He couldn't tell what it was, but it looked even bigger than some of the creatures that stayed deep in the darkness, taking trophies when the mood struck them. The hybrid remembered a situation where he had been pursuing a blue whale. He was nearly upon the ninety-foot creature when it suddenly vanished as something that crossed its path took it completely into its mouth. All the leviathan saw were blotches on the thing's flank. He had no desire to be dessert and sped off in the other direction from the colossal thing that had stolen his meal.

The panel closed and the huge form settled onto the sea bed. The hybrid inspected it from a respectful distance.

He couldn't discern its full length since it was curled up into an oblong. Its skin looked uneven, as if it had been beset upon by barnacles, with scars revealing past battles. He saw no tail flukes, and closer observing revealed a strange mouth. Instead of a top and a bottom, it had four sides, each marked by protruding teeth. And despite its posture, the leviathan detected something that indicated the creature was still alive —not a heartbeat, but a spark of neuronic activity deep within. The thing looked dead, yet it still lived.

The leviathan approached cautiously, reaching out a tentacle to poke the huge creature.

The barnacled thing immediately recoiled, thrashed, and revealed itself.

It was a long, snaking thing with four flippers, and dwarfed the leviathan. The creature's eyes were glazed and probably were not designed for the darkness, but it was fast and very nearly caught the tentacle. It whipped its head toward the leviathan and opened its mouth.

The four sides of the mouth opened simultaneously, like the blooming of some unholy deep-water anemone, and snapped shut. It slowly lifted its body from the sea floor and, with sudden speed, barreled in his direction.

The leviathan was quicker and managed to avoid the rush, but the wake from the thing's attack pushed him into an awkward roll. Just as he reoriented himself, the new foe was nearly upon him.

The leviathan avoided the snapping jaws and dove for the deeper dark. He would take the fight to this new invader there, or even deeper. He'd only explored the deepest dark once, and it was the first time he'd ever known fear.

This was a close second; he had to weave and dodge the thing, which managed to stay uncomfortably close on his tail, jaws snapping on empty water. The snatches of light disappeared by turns as the two creatures dove deeper. Soon they were completely enveloped in darkness. The leviathan released its ink cloud to confuse its pursuer.

It was a critical error in tactics.

The beast with the four jaws homed in on the cloud and seized the hybrid by the tail, stopping the leviathan's progress. Suckered tentacles deployed, fastening on and removing an eye from the huge predator. The pursuer's teeth punctured the leviathan's tail from all sides, piercing but not severing.

The hybrid thrashed and tried to bite its captor but could not bend its body far enough to reach the larger creature. The giant monster shook the smaller like a terrier would a rat.

Suddenly, when the hybrid thought its reign was over, its adversary released him and sped away, making for the deepest dark and the horrors within.

The leviathan, puzzled over its release, neared a plateau on one of the many sea mountains. An unfamiliar sensation overwhelmed him. His conditioning to hunt winked out and he settled on the plateau. He closed his eyes and the head light extinguished.

Far below the huge creature was having its way with the many species that dwelt in areas nothing else dared go.

Prehistoric throwbacks twisted by the refuse of humanity, hybrid travesties that made the leviathan on the plateau look normal, smaller creatures that preyed in packs so large that they dwarfed even the largest creatures in the depths, all fell to this hideous trespasser. Some ended up inside it, processed as sustenance. Others were treated as the hybrid was, bitten and left to slumber. When it had done its work, the giant creature swam back to the structure and waited in the shadows just beyond the reach of the ineffective lights.

Their slumber ended when the infection took root.

One by one their eyes flicked open, slaves to something that replaced their autonomy. Dead, yet still living. By ones, then twos, they formed a school and followed the trail that the monster had laid for them. The tentacled leviathan joined them as they passed, taking its place among the throwbacks and mutants that homed in on the structure.

The massed and transformed sea creatures easily overwhelmed the defenses of the structure. Smaller reanimated creatures breeched small external openings and made short work of the beings inside the structure. The last being managed to press a button that initiated a self-destruct protocol before the small creatures whose mouths took up three fourths of their length ripped his body into chum. The explosion scattered the school of monsters to the currents, stunning them. Their bodies settled in different pockets of the sea, some of them waking in waters so cold that some of them immediately froze. Others found themselves in areas where salt met fresh, and their body chemistry worked feverishly to strike a balance.

But one by one they awoke from their stunned states and immediately began to prowl in clearer waters unimpeded by darkness. Their prey was slower and more arrogant, believing that they ruled the sea. By increments, the relocated zombie fish fed, and then spread the infection.

As was usually the case, humanity was too slow on the uptake to realize what was happening. The first reports came from Japan, where sushi had suddenly started making people sick. The rumors of quick deaths followed by reanimation were ignored, passed off as clickbait or drug-fueled ramblings. But, soon, people started believing. The reanimated serving of tuna poke that attacked its eater on national television clinched things. Millions saw it initially, the bright pink flesh covered with spicy mayonnaise forcing itself en mass down the influencer's throat, her eyes turning back in her head as the pieces burrowed down her throat and then burst from her belly. By the time reactions to the video turned to action, it was too late.

The tentacled leviathan found itself in temperate waters around a Pacific Island chain, and when it took up residence things began to change. Toxins leeched off its body, contaminating everything from plankton and coral to sustenance fish. Nothing was spared. Larger species consumed the smaller, and subsequently transformed into creatures like the leviathan, existing within a liminal space somewhere between dead and living. As the island inhabitants and those who visited the island, mined and consumed the sea's bounty, they started to change as well. The fortunate died and did not resurrect. The other effects ranged from regressing to primitive savagery to dying and resurrecting as ravenous creatures afflicted with a disease that resembled bulimia. It wasn't long before the contagion on the island moved to the mainland, and those that had somehow managed to avoid the contagion took to the sea in whatever sorts of craft they could salvage. Some situated themselves on great platforms that survived the elements; others found themselves marooned on cruise ships whose resources were finite. The crafts were easy prey, in many cases the survivors turned upon each other over the few resources left, and reverted to primitivism without being infected.

Despite the mounting evidence, those with power and safety declared the upheaval in the oceans to be isolated experiences and urged the survivors to trust in the lord and the government's ability to handle things. Humanity's hubris lasted until the rivers and lakes in the landlocked areas became infested, and, finally, the leviathan found himself in a world teeming with the infected, searching neverendingly for sustenance. The contaminant discouraged the infected species from cannibalizing each other and, eventually, the infected began to waste away from starvation. The leviathan was one of the last remaining sea creatures; it left the temperate waters and swam, drawn by something that it didn't understand back to the depths it had inhabited. The remains of the structure were still standing, and there it found the creature that had started it all, once again curled up against the top of a sea mount.

The leviathan sensed only a weak glimmer of life within the giant creature, and wasted no time in carving a huge chunk from the creature's flank. Thousands of smaller creatures flocked to the gash, schooling back and forth within the gushing blood and floating scraps of flesh. The creature was soon fully consumed; not even bones remained

The well-nourished leviathan, having fed well, dove towards the darkest depths; refreshed, and fearless, ready to conquer what was left of the sea and install itself as a new ruler.

Vibrissae

by Irena Barbara Nagler

Snow cat on a picnic table
through twig whiskers
palpates the sentient
air. Uncoils her snow-tail,
Begins to stalk, awakening
with her tread the pockets
of magick. They split open, releasing
living fields.

A hawk in enclosure
flaps mortally injured wings. Not far away
its flown self perches in the bones of a woman
who stands on a path, then whirls, cloud-gazing.

Into a fold, dark & pulsing
the hawk launches itself
carrying seeds of fire
in search of open skies.

The winter-white blanket is witness.

The hawk-woman rubs her eyes. Where was she just now?
She pulls out her phone to forget.

The other birds are restless too now, rustling in their hutches.
The snow cat returns to her table.
Her white blanket settles around her. That perfect curling tail.

We may never know how many creatures walk here
or claw open universal tunnels
as the world expands in increments of snow.

Into the starwood

by Irena Barbara Nagler

She fell, her pelage of red-gold velvet
draped over concrete, facing the woods.

now
after the roar and snap, exploding inner kingdom, blood and bone
a life slammed shut
the deer with a red tear etched into her face
is climbing the hill forest
up and up into the starwood.

The starwood wraps around us
a womb-companion
its contours matching the city.
It glitters in the spaces
between urban branches.

The eternal dance of wolves and deer
flames on velvet night.

Sometimes, in the hour before dawn
you part curtains of rain
and enter into the starwood

and wake again later,
having mostly forgotten
walking in the tree of your bones

the place where stars and deer
dine together on shining leaves.

Air Strike In No Man's Land

by Tamara Kaye Sellman

(A version of this story previously appeared as a syllabic poem form for the WildSound poetry festival in August 2025)

Wings flash. Between this theater of needled trees, the woodpecker cruises, its nose precise as the tip of a rocket, its red crest behind sharp eyes fierce and jagged. It reaches the deadwood trunk, no longer a tree anymore, its ragged top blackened where its towering branches were burned to sticks and ash during last fall's firestorm.

The woodpecker remembers. Entire leaps of flame razed this bank of hundred-foot hemlocks to stubble. After the lightning that set the wildfire, a cloudburst dumped an inch of rain an hour over the mountain until flames withered to streamers of smoke.

Now, the woodpecker knows that, as it lands, the devastated stump's loose silvered bark will explode under its taloned grip to reveal a feast of insects.

The nation of termites beneath have spent the fall swamping the dead trees, mining their inner whorls of pith, cellulose, and gum. They rebuild, reroute, masticate, digest all the elements of this organism in its various stages of decomposition. They build networks of tunnels, mate, defecate in this palatial nest afforded them by divine calamity.

The woodpecker ratchets its torpedo-like beak into the tree's spongey heartwood, capturing entire precincts of termites within seconds. Those deeply embedded brandish their pincer mouthparts in self-defense, their segments quivering until the woodpecker's hammering strike flays them lifeless against rotten fiber. The automatic staccato of the bird's incessant chisel deafens and vibrates the resolve of an entire colony.

The termites along the perimeter exterior eject themselves, tumble into the litter of the deep woods' floor, avoiding the terror of the bird's razor beak, the hostile penetration of its claws into the fragile pith where clumps of their glistening honey-colored eggs will fall to the bird's violent feeding. These insects chance it for a soft landing in the underground of leaves and lichen that serve as a bunker for regrouping and subterranean reconnaissance. No hard feelings, only heads down, lines formed. There will be more eggs to lay, more fiber to macerate with their bile, to chew into sustenance, more crosscuts to dig, until this last gasp of a tree is nothing but sawdust.

And then, as quickly as it soared through this glen glowing in amber October light, it is as quickly dispatched in a seizure: golden leatherette along the joints of a Cooper's hawk's legs, so swift in its attack that even the termites do not sense it coming. The stealthy bird of prey grapples its red-crested hostage noiselessly. An explosion of underbelly down from both birds floats like dead leaves. They levitate in the moment when the forest as witness pauses to hold its breath, until it heaves a sigh, setting loose the feathers to snowfall over the exoskeletons of unsuspecting termites.

The woodpecker, stricken, rattles its shrill call until the hawk clamps its claws around its neck, squeezing, wringing, breaking red into startled silence. It feels the expulsion of termite bodies from its gullet during this, its final breath.

Wildfires Worry the Scarecrow

by LindaAnn LoSchiavo

A crackle of illicit energy
Alarmed the scarecrow who considers fire,
An allegory of endangerment
To souls, as human recklessness writ large.

Across the ridge, a pungent orange sky
Is fuming, taunting forests, farms, and fields.

What's next? Ruination? The collapsed cornstalks,
Majestic grains ploughed down? Their dry exile?

Hot embers, breeze tossed, could ignite birds' nests,
Increasing wind's blind beg for reaper light.

"No future when you're going up in flames,"
He thinks, aware of crickets' rattle-hum.

Dust clouds rise. Has the cavalry arrived?

Tall power line poles, having been trees once,
Remind Straw Man about his unused wish
That Mother Nature gave when he was made.

What if ...? What if he'd split into varied
Dissimilar formations, each equipped

With a fire hose – extinguishing the force
That overheats the Earth. Is that enough?

Unknown to him, imperious ghosts laugh.

Great Blue on Swan Lake

by Tracy Thompson

He glides and swoops
to land near shore,
prehistoric wings fanning closed at his sides.
He is stealth.

Slowly, one backward-hinged footstep at a time,
he scouts the water ahead.
Somehow, those eyes at the top of that accordion neck
can spot that flash of protein beneath the surface,
can calculate the refraction,
can launch that deadly beak with absolute precision
to spear a tasty morsel.

He is perfectly suited to his task.

Just Endings

by Elad Haber

Surprisingly, the mermaid girl survived. Wet and wounded, but alive.

*

In another part of the forest, a fire raged. Its tongues were long tendrils of flames. Its fists clobbered trees and sent animals screaming. Its maw growled in fury. Burning leaves fell like rain, caught in the wind and spreading.

The foolish men playing at war, with their flaming arrows and balls of tar, fled the forest as fast as their cowardly legs could take them.

There had been a village there amongst the trees. Huts and pits and charred remains.

The hungry fire feasted for days, crumbling bits of forest in its teeth, then finally satiated, it rested. Plumes of black smoke drifted into the sky. In the quiet dark of an early morning, when the smoke was only whispers left on the burned ground, a glow emerged from underneath dead trees. It was a ball of light, dimmed in despair at the destruction around it. It darted between various parts of the ruined forest, searching.

In the remnants of the village, the light found something. A boy—dead, of course, but in one piece due to the cover of his half-buried home.

The ball burrowed into him. A glow emanated from the boy's chest, strong at first, then fainter and fainter. When the light was finally gone altogether, the boy coughed. Ash flew out of his mouth and nose.

The boy pushed through a narrow gap in the wreckage around him into the weak daylight. His clothes had been burned in the flames. The village he knew was dark smudges on scorched earth. His eyes lingered on the bodies, skeletal remains, blackened by fire. Looking at them, he didn't feel anything. There was nothing left here. So, he started walking.

Often, endings are actually beginnings.

*

The mermaid pushed aside a clump of wet, red hair.

She was draped on a boulder at the center of a clearing. Puddles in the crevices of the rock surrounded her. Trees of various configurations watched her from all sides —sycamore, fir, pine, as if this forest was made of pieces of all the forests in the world.

She was naked. Her breasts hung free, her middle exposed, and her tail was badly injured. She tried to push herself up, but her body wailed in pain. Even sliding a little to the side lanced pain through her back and shoulders. She couldn't quite remember the watery crash that stranded her on this rock, but she must have landed on her left side. E very muscle on that side was a dagger of pain, glass-cracking across the rest of her body. She couldn't move her midsection. She used her right arm to grab some leaves and moss to cover her exposed tail.

The girl stared at the changing sky —the rise and fall of the harsh golden sun. At first, it felt strange on her bare skin, hot and uncomfortable. But after a while, she welcomed the warmth, especially after a cold night. The nights were tough. Strange sounds reverberated from the trees, and she waited in horror for some animal to find and attack her.

But nothing and no one came. It was as if her clearing were a bubble, and although she could hear creatures on the other side, none of them entered. She was safe—and lonely.

Days passed in silence. Weeks, perhaps.

She wondered about her bubble. This forest was clearly large. Why did she end up here, in this clearing? Was some fate awaiting her? Her father used to talk about "nature's destiny," but she stopped herself from remembering more. Memories are wounds, in the right light. She didn't need to eat or drink due to the magic inside of her, an echo of her family's Guardian genealogy, imbued with knowledge of the world beyond even her ocean.

Without anything else to do, she closed her eyes and began to sing. It was a sad song. Her voice was beautiful, full of passion, but the sound was swallowed in tears. It emerged out of her thin frame as if her whole life composed a dirge.

*

The boy hid from the light. The sun's rays poked through holes in the canopy of trees and threatened to expose him. To what, he wasn't sure. The forest seemed empty save for him, but he was nonetheless afraid.

He wandered the forest with no destination in mind, just *away*. Away from the sizzling earth of his village. Away from the world that betrayed him. He walked for an entire day until darkness fell and his stomach rumbled and his bare feet ached.

The canopy was thick here, and the forest was so dark he couldn't see even a few inches ahead of him.

He felt something stirring in his chest. He looked down to see it alight. The light was faint, but enough. He rose, glowing, and began to walk again. He felt no fear from the light, not even any self-reflective curiosity. It was as if the light were an old friend and its presence was comforting.

It was then that he heard the sound. At first, he thought it was the beginning of another forest fire, and his heart started beating faster. But it wasn't angry or threatening. Instead, it was a kind of wailing, a melody somewhere buried in the wave of sound.

He turned towards it. The sound grew louder as he approached so he picked up his pace until he was breathing heavy and so close that he could hear her clearly now.

The blue haze of morning arrived, toying with colors, and his chest's light receded. He could make out a clearing behind a row of trees. Something moving. He hesitated.

He heard a call from the clearing: "Who goes there?" the voice demanded.

The boy walked into the light.

*

She stopped singing as soon as she heard the rustling from beyond the trees. She had been singing for hours, so her brain was woozy, her vision unfocused.

She shook her head to snap herself back to reality. Whatever person or animal lurked in the shadows, they were waiting. Stalking. One of her hands balled into a fist and she called out. She cursed herself for not fashioning some kind of weapon after all this time.

But it was just a boy who emerged from the trees—naked as a baby, with a slightly swollen belly, dark skin, and cuts and bruises on his bare feet.

The girl exhaled.

She put her arm on her chest to cover her bare breasts and adjusted the carpet of moss on her midsection.

"It's okay," she said to the boy. "I won't hurt you."

He took a few tentative steps forward.

"What's your name?" she asked.

He shook his head.

"It's okay," she said again. "Are you thirsty?"

The boy didn't answer, but he came a little bit closer to her rock.

The girl looked around the clearing and pointed at a palm tree. There was a cluster of low hanging coconuts. "There," she told him, pointing. "Can you get me one of those?"

The boy was hesitant to follow her directions, but after a moment walked to where she pointed. He climbed up the tree and pulled down a brown globe. He was afraid to step too close to her, so he threw the coconut at her. His distrust made her smile.

She examined the fruit, found the right spot, and slammed it against the good-for-almost-nothing rock. The fruit split open, a little bit of water spilling out, and then she held both sides out to the boy.

Still tentative, but relaxing,the boy stepped closer and grabbed one half and immediately set it to his lips to drink. He looked up at her after, his face bright. She extended the other half, and he took it and drank it all, coughing a little after.

"Good, right?" she said, smiling. He grinned and nodded.

The boy stared at her for a moment. He looked around with some kind of inspiration and then grabbed the two coconut halves and slipped behind the rock, fiddling with something the girl couldn't see. After a few minutes, he straightened up and handed her back the coconuts, but tied with a few thin branches so it formed a makeshift bra.

She laughed. "Thank you," she said and looked down at his small and exposed penis. "Now find something for yourself."

*

The boy was curious and often funny. He climbed every disparate tree in the clearing, gathered fruit and seeds and branches of different shapes and colors. He laid those on the rock near the girl, and she directed him, using hand gestures, which he mimicked in exaggerated ways.

Over time, she taught him language. He grew in leaps and bounds over the course of that first year—from a seedling to a small tree, hair wild and uncouth like her own, his eyes and belly always hungry, his mouth just starting to put together sounds into words. He built himself a hut near the rock where he slept.

Mostly, he was curious about her. The moss blanket she used to cover the bottom half of her body had started to meld with the rock, to dig with its green fingers into the stone, pinning her in place. The bottom half of the rock had formed into a bulbous, broken mound resembling an upside-down Y.

The first time she showed the boy her ruined tail, a dark red gash through the sparkling blue scales, the boy cried out as if the injury had just happened. He grabbed as many crude tools he could to try and help, maybe stitch her body back together again.

The girl shook her head and calmed him down. How could she explain to him how long it had been since she got hurt? She wasn't even sure, herself. Weeks, maybe years, maybe decades. Time had moved in a glacial pace before the boy arrived, but things were happening fast now.

The boy learned to talk.

"Tell me," he said, slowly pronouncing the words, "why are you here?"

He asked every day, and she turned away instead of answering, until one day, she sighed and told him the story.

"We lived in a palace under the sea," she said, wiping the first of many tears from her cheeks. "We called it La Mer. It was a place of beauty and song. I was one of a dozen daughters to the Sea King, tasked with protecting an underwater archipelago. Then, one day, a great storm ravaged the sea, grabbing and pulling our precious water away as if a thirsty god was drinking it all up. I watched as cyclones ravaged the spires and towers of my palace, killing my sisters and my beloved father. Then a cyclone came for me. It pulled me out of the water, spinning me around for what felt like hours, taking me far away from the sea, and then dropping me here, on this rock, forever."

He couldn't understand the words or the imagery behind them. He had never seen the sea. But his eyes were kind and sad. He took her hand and squeezed it with all his might.

*

Years passed.

The boy grew to an imposing figure, lean and muscled, feral in his movements, unwashed hair on his head and chest, but his face was bare, boyish. He learned to hunt for the small animals around the clearing, cooked them up, used their skin for clothes and bones for tools.

As for the girl, she hadn't aged, but she looked different. She had been on the rock for a lifetime and the stone had consumed so much of her. The moss that once covered her bottom half had mixed with dirt and sediment to form a heavy layer. It was moving upwards, a tiny bit every day. She felt it around her stomach now, but she knew it was coming for the rest of her.

Their life together was quiet, almost mundane. The boy spent most of his day finding food, hunting, cooking (although fire still scared him, she could tell), cleaning up after himself, and repairing various parts of his improvised home. She watched him as he worked, occasionally calling out advice.

Just as he did to her, she prodded him about his past. And just like her, he didn't want to talk about it. Every once in a while, a flare of light filled the clearing, and when she asked him about it, he shook his head. Then she asked again and again, until, finally, one cold night while they shivered together, he seemed to relax, fully, bodily and completely, relax, and his chest glowed, warming them. He allowed himself a smile and then, without her asking, he spoke. He told her about waking up in the burned village and the glow from his chest, a strange but comforting feeling. He recalled feeling so lost and afraid and then… a voice.

He scooted up the rock a little so she could rest her head on his sharp shoulder.

Later that evening, she sang

It was her familiar sad song, continuous except for a moment's pause while she caught her breath, and a gruff voice carried on the wind. The boy opened his eyes and looked at her. She'd heard it too.

As the men approached, the boy began breathing heavily. The girl whispered calming words despite her own fear.

The brush around the border trees shifted as footsteps trampled the ground. There was a half dozen of them, tall and terrifying, holding torches which cast wild shadows on their bodies. Their heads were shaved and they had tattoos on their faces. Bird feathers covered their clothes so they looked like hybrid animals: half man, half *thing*.

Suspiciously, they scanned the clearing, at the frightened boy and the half-naked girl on the rock. A few of them sneered.

The boy balled his fists and gathered his courage and then sprang forward, his arms flailing. Two of the intruders grabbed him and held him down.

The men holding the boy down nodded at the girl and motioned for others to grab her.

"No!" shouted the boy. "Leave her alone!"

He looked at the girl. Her face was ashen as the intruders began to climb her rock. They locked eyes. She took a long breath, then let it out, a burst of air that extinguished all of their torches. The world went dark.

The boy gritted his teeth and let his glow shine. A burst of white light emanated from his chest, timid at first, then bright and hanging high in the sky. The intruders stared at it in disbelief. Then the light blinded them, a flash that illuminated the world. In that instant, the boy struck. He unsheathed two daggers from his captors' belts and used their own weapons to slice their throats. He lunged forward and embedded the blades in another man's stomach. As the man fell, he dropped a sword, and the boy picked it up and held it up high, the light from his chest snaking out like vines to the weapon and engulfing it in white light. He lowered the sword and used it to cut through the remaining men.

Only the girl's terrified gasps could be heard in the forest silence.

By the time the white light faded, the ground was stained red and the man, no longer a boy, wheezed beside her rock, blood in his eyes and blood on his chest, and nothing was ever the same again.

*

After that night, he didn't sleep much. When he did close his eyes for a bit, he had bad dreams— of tattoos and infernos. He woke up, thrashing and screaming and almost capsized his little house.

She didn't need sleep, just as she didn't need food or water or other human necessities, but she often rested in a kind of meditative haze. When she opened her eyes from that calming state, she often didn't recognize the angry man stalking around their clearing, frightened of shadows.

"Hi," she ventured.

He looked up, but didn't respond.

He kept things from the intruders—knives and swords and something that looked like a wooden tool. He stripped their bodies and stole their clothes. He was no longer the bare-chested man of the woods. His long hair rested on a bloodied red jacket and he wore dark pants and kept two blades on him at all times.

She didn't sing anymore.

He was roasting up a small creature, and the crackling of the fire was loud in the silence of the clearing. He was muttering to himself.

"What did you say?" she asked.

This time, he responded. "I need to do something. Something about *them.*"

"Them?" she parroted, although she knew.

"Men," he spat, spittle igniting the fire below him. "They are a menace." He closed his eyes and grimaced at

some image in his head. "They're responsible. The fire. The death of my village. I can see them now, playing at war. Flaming arrows. Balls of fire."

She felt suddenly cold. "How can you know that?"

Now he looked reverent, touching the grass beside his feet like a lover's caress. "The Guardian of the forest is inside of me. The forest demands action."

"Where will you go?"

"Their cities and towns. I will find them and make them answer for their crimes."

"And what about me?" she asked him.

He looked up from his cooking and stared at her.

"The forest will protect you," he said. "I know it will."

His task forgotten, he climbed up the rock to lay his head on her lap as he did when he was just a boy. The angry face he wore moments ago washed away, temporarily. "I love you," he said to her. "But I must do this. For my family. For you. For the forest."

She stroked his hair. "You might die," she said.

"Yes."

"And I'll never see you again."

"Yes."

"So then stay!" Her voice rose in despair. "Stay and live here with me like we used to. We'll sing and be together and be safe here."

He rose and his mouth twisted into a frown. "I cannot. I will place some traps in the trees, just in case. But I must go. I must enact my birthright."

"Your birthright?"

His chest glowed. "It's what I was made for. *Justice."*

*

The sun and the moon played their endless game of hide and seek. More years passed in a blur of silence and pain.

The girl was engulfed in rock. It covered her chest, leaving only a few slivers of skin in various parts of her upper body. The rock was heavy and green with moss. It continued to spread, sending out thin sinews of stone to wrap around her shoulders and begin its conquest of her arms. Wisps of grey were visible in her hair.

*

The first time he came back, he was full of life, bursting with stories of people and cities beyond the forest, of fathers and daughters and sons and lovers. At first, he watched them from the shadows of streets and alehouses, shy and nervous about his speech.

"But you taught me well," he said to her. "I found my confidence and courage to speak to strangers. And once I got started, I couldn't stop. I worked in whatever job I could find to get some coins for food and a place to sleep. I spoke to everyone and they told me their stories."

He looked much different now. He cut his long hair but let a beard grow so his face was partially hidden. He noticed her staring at it and rubbed a hand on the scratchy surface.

"I know," he said. "Most of the men have beards, so I wanted to fit in, but it's itchy. I don't like it."

"I want to see your face," she said to him.

He retrieved a thin razor from a bag full of strange objects. He went away to fill some water and when he got back, he sat on the rock facing her.

Slowly, with her limited movements due to the rock, she shaved his beard while he continued to tell her about the world outside the forest. When she was done, she wet a rag and used it to clean his face.

She smiled at him, recognizing the boy in the man's face. He smiled back, but then a dark countenance appeared, tinging his cheeks in sadness.

"There were bad men, too," he told her. "Thieves and rapists and murderers. I dealt with them, like I told you I would."

She nodded. "Good," she said.

He kept his eyes cast downward, unable to lock eyes with her.

After some silence, she said, "You are going back."

"Yes."

"When?"

"Soon, but not right away."

He looked up at her. His eyes were wet and swollen. There were no more words that night. He lay down next to her on the rock, and even though the surface was rough, he slept beside her.

*

The next time he came back, he brought oils and potions. He was older now, grizzled and graying. His dark skin was even darker in parts, like bruises that never healed.

"For the pain," he said.

She was mostly stone now. It had attacked her shoulders and solidified her arms so that only her wrists and hands were flesh. It gripped her neck and had started digging into her cheeks.

He opened the small bottles and powders and mixed them together how he had been shown and then used the tip of his finger to gently massage whatever skin he could find. The smell was nice, but it didn't do much for the pain.

Besides, she didn't feel much anymore. The rock had claimed most of her body, and with it, her pain receptors. She felt only numbness in what once was her body and now felt more like her grave.

"I don't have long now," she said. "I wish. . . ." she trailed off without finishing her thought.

He looked into her eyes. "Tell me."

"It's silly. I know it won't happen. I just wish... I could see the ocean one more time. Or at least, know it's there. That it survived."

A small grin formed on his face. "It is," he said quietly. Then, louder, "I swear to you it is. I saw it. I journeyed to the far end of the continent. I saw an endless ocean that no storm could destroy."

She was crying then. "Thank you," she said.

His expression turned grim, from a smile to stone serious. He shifted and pulled a long sword from his belt and placed it on the rock.

"What is that for?" she asked.

"Mercy," he told her.

More tears fell.

She spoke to prolong the moment. "I thought you only believed in justice."

He shook his head. "I've seen the world now. And I was wrong. There is no justice here or anywhere." He reached out to touch her stone flesh. "Just endings."

Avalanche

by Shane David Morin

A howl of primacy. Whether
It arises from winter winds or wolves,
I can't tell. Maybe it's the damned weather,
This avalanching snow, slowly evolving

Into a new tundra around an ice castle catacomb,
Sculpting to the contours of cedar cabin.
Some say time stands still, freezes even, while
Quiet groans grow from walls, a daze

Falls upon me as collapsed rooves, rhythms of hooves
Stampede along peripheral hearing,
Doors creak as screw-topped Vermouth,
Fireplace rages, embers crackle, searing

My tongue, viscous blood pumping,
thumpingalongtheventricles
RagingRaginginmybrainthethumpingthumpinginmyearscircl
esconcentric
Thewallscreepclosercreakingshrieking(oristhatme?)thebreathi
ngunder
Rooftopsresonatessilenceandheartbeatandthebreathingthebre
athing—

by Shane David Morin

Obsidian roses blossom among the rot,
Spindle among fresh topsoil, thread through
The cypress 3 by 6, buried with yesterdays,
Vacant prayers mumbled under drunken breath,
My utterings muffled by earth and coffin.

There's a silence that stifles vibrancy,
Threads severed by neglect and expectation,
A one-way road we speed down towards
The end, which is the beginning, which is

To say falling in reverse only serves
The inevitable collision, while you
run in regression, destination unknown

'cause it was never me, really. Perhaps
A body to stave off abandonment or
To keep the voices from consuming yours.

I lay imperfectly decaying, growing
Obsidian roses from collapsed capillaries,
Hoping you'll pluck petals to spread

Across the empty bed you share
With the conflagration of memories gifted

Before I was cast aside as a dying rose.

by Shane David Morin

Long have I slumbered
Dreaming away the passing days
Shape-shifting, a restless woman encumbered

I shall arise, climb from this caldera
An emptiness I called home
Reignite myself Chimera
Seek love I'll never know

How I burn for thee,
My Glorious! My Wahieloa!
I shall embrace (and be embraced)
Until we witness the drying of the seas

I rage that I cannot caress your face
Flee to the brethren Samoa

Return to exact my vengeance
Bringer of Wrath
Scorch the ground you find precious
Bury all human semblance, rain fire endless
Linger on the path
I will arise as igneous crashes, laying a trail of ash

I burn
Fuming in jealousy
I return
Restoring the earth's felicity

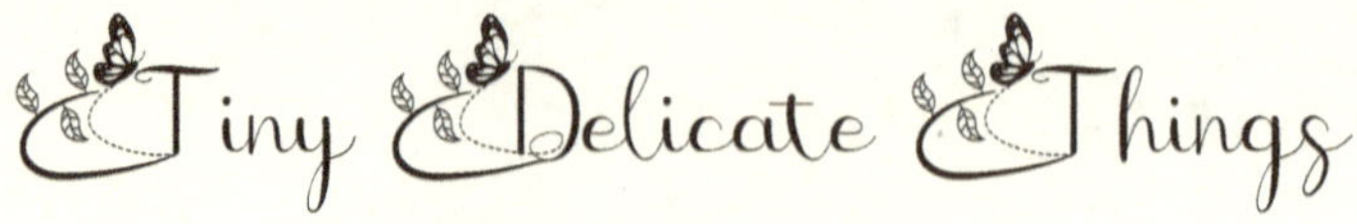

Tiny Delicate Things

by Stacy Schonhardt

Her screams woke me from a dead sleep. I rubbed the crust from my eyes and smelled the copper-saltwater blood before I saw it. Drips dotted the floor near the bedroom. Streaks and smears blotched the hallway.

I called her name, but she didn't answer. I heard her deep, guttural moan and heavy footsteps pacing up and down the wood floors. She was visibly frightened when I found her. The previous births had been fairly easy, but something was very, very wrong this time.

She tried to run from me, and I caught her in the kitchen. For a moment, I blocked her from leaving the room. I could just see the top of a tiny head protruding from between her legs. She cried out in pain and pushed past me, scrambling into the living room. There she collapsed on the floor, her huge belly heaving with each contraction.

I sat next to her, as I had before, and tried to help ease the baby into the world. His head was too big to easily pass through her opening. As she pushed him out, I was horrified to see his little belly had ripped open, and his intestines were spilling out like tiny worms. He didn't bleed—he was already dead —but the way he came into the world made my stomach churn. The sight of him coming apart at the umbilicus is burned into the inside of my eyelids. I still see it sometimes at night.

I petted her and consoled her, and in a few slick minutes, the second one came out. It wiggled and squeaked wetly in my hands. I was grateful for that scrappy bit of life. Three was still fetal. Its pale skin felt like a wet olive. Mercifully, it never moved or took a breath. So small it fit into my palm. It never had a chance. Four's abdomen was split open like One's.

The father of her babies was afraid, hiding in the living room. Coward. He was young and kind of stupid, but she didn't have high standards. I didn't know about the stereotype about orange ones then. He had some extra fingers and toes, big blue eyes, and the kind of long hair that matted easily and often.

About four hours in, my other roommate climbed up the three flights of stairs to our home. He started to wiggle the lock, but I rushed over to stop him.

Through the closed door I yelled, "She's in labor!"

He mumbled back, "Oh, wonderful!"

I paused. "No. No, it's not wonderful. Most of them are stillborn. I don't know what's going on, but it's pretty bad. You don't want to see this. You don't want this trauma. Go down the street and get me a bottle of vodka, leave it outside the door, and go to the cafe or something. I'll call you later."

He brought me the booze and left.

I mixed myself up a pitcher with some orange juice to numb some of the horror.

I didn't call him later.

He came home well after midnight. He helped mop up the fluids, wrap the dead, and dig some tiny little graves in the backyard of our rental.

Five and Six were born the next day, both alive. They were the last of that litter. Six was born with his front paws bent the wrong way. I managed as best I could with bandages and cotton swab splints to slowly and gently pull them around.

Five died three days later when she dropped him on his head. He was the only one with any color to him. I think he would have been a gray tabby.

The only babies that survived were Two and Six. Within a few weeks, they both were romping around, and Six's paws looked normal.

I should have kept Six. I should have kept both him and Two. They were adorable. All white, like their mom. They snuggled and nursed and bounced around the apartment. Small, delicate little things. I placed an ad and gave them to good homes, as one does.

I felt horrible the whole time. It was my fault. I should have scraped together money to prevent it somehow. I was so worried that she'd retained some membranes or placenta, that she'd get sick.

I tried. I did what I could. I was broke, and had sometimes gone without to make sure she had food. I don't remember seeing blood everywhere, but I remember smelling it, smelling the birth of the dead kittens. It smelled like copper and seashore and fear. I'm not sure whose fear. I remember the bitter taste of the cheap vodka and the orange juice and my own tears. Looking back on it now, a lifetime later, I keep seeking absolution.

Not this birth, but the next, killed her. She gave birth to a healthy litter, all of them cute and squirmy, some white, some orange. The father was the same male cat. I don't know why my roommate hadn't gotten him neutered by then. And then she developed an infection before the babies were weaned. Something that made her bleed.

By then my roommate and I had split up. He moved out while she was pregnant, but we decided to remain friends. I begged and borrowed money from friends and family to take her to the vet.

She was prescribed antibiotics, but every time I got one down her throat, she'd spit it out. Like she was done even trying to survive. She was so weak, I knew her time was close.

Rent was too high for me to stay alone in that apartment, and I moved too. I asked my former roommate if I could bring her and her babies over to his place, so I would be spared having her die in my new apartment the first night I was there. He agreed, and everyone was scooped into a box and brought over to his place. I stayed up as long as I could, but I was already exhausted from packing and carrying boxes. I finally fell asleep, and she took that as a cue. She died early that morning on his kitchen floor, her eyes open, her mouth wide in a scream.

Some friends who lived out of town on a farm offered me a place to bury her and some shots of something strong and clear afterward. Most of that night is a blur, but I remember them loaning me their kid and a shovel to dig. And wrapping her like an infant in her favorite sweatshirt of mine. I think it was orange. I don't know why I had an orange sweatshirt. I look sickly in orange. And her eyes were still open, I couldn't close them. And the dirt falling on her face in the deep hole.

Sun In My Darkness

by Sacha Rosel

At first it's imperceptible, vines whirling round my ankles like multiple bracelets. Hungering for contact, it's only natural for you to reach out and waltz your gratitude onto my ticklish skin: I've been studying you, probing into your tiniest hairy pods for seeds to germinate and nodes to prowl. Only these tentative strands frolicking between my feet have emerged so far, but more are bound to come, prolific as you are. Heavy with waiting, I fall asleep, knowing my patient tending to your flourishing will soon have its reward.

I blink once, twice, and suddenly you're everywhere: vine-braided cornucopia exploding upwards and downwards, a ballroom of roots lassoing their way deep into the soil where nutrients hide, then rabidly swaying back to come up for air and reproduce again and again. I see the ground now pulsing trifoliate, viridian-bright, shrouding the entire length of the laboratory as far as the eyes can reach.

Clawing away all other sparks of vegetation from your path, you alter, spoil and then triumph, becoming the only one left standing. But that's the beauty of your species, isn't it? Aggressive, uncontrollable, leeching on every dirt particle, every water drop your ravenous roots might divine in the surrounding area, because you can't coexist with anything but your own image. In this respect, you're very similar to us. Has anyone ever told you —susurrating flossy human sounds into your pods so as to give them strength, or perhaps stop them for fear you might conquer the whole world?

And what's there to fear really, when all we've ever done was conquering and leeching on all the bounties this planet could possibly offer? Are we to flee a creature who behaves like us—ceaselessly taking without asking, enduring by erasing everything in sight—or bow down in recognition, its undeterred marching a mirror of our own glory?

Colleagues used to warn me, mouthing the word which spells your name cautiously, almost imperceptibly *—kudzu —* as if it was a curse or something to avoid like the plague. I'd never paid heed to their whispers. Superstition is not something to be welcomed when you are a scientist. Observation, that's my only guiding star, and the will to absorb as much as possible from the plants I study, because in studying them, I can see our own selves magnified and rejoice at the discovery.

Of course, I knew you would fuse with the soil and other plants, possibly also with the cables and wires trailing and climbing all over the lab, themselves looking more and more like perennial vines—anything to let your ecstatic dance of expansion rage on unstoppable. In fact, I was looking forward to celebrating your full-scale invasion as a testimony to the vital wish to annihilate and persist, the only instinct allowing a species to survive evolution and bend it to its will. We humans did the same with all the other living, breathing things. Why should you behave differently?

I didn't know you would end up dancing inside me too, though.

Again like small tendrils, your vines graze against my skin, scraping for possible cavities. Ill with love for proliferation, you are here to conquer and explode your mighty seeds into my feeble shell. *Aggressiveness becomes you—* my mind gulps in awe as you flog your way into my flesh, and something deep inside me suddenly caves in as if this was happening to somebody else, as if it was simply an experiment, myself the alpha and the omega of the ultimate scientific adventure. I can't say no to you but adore you and your strategy of conquest. So I welcome all your arms made of roots as they come, flaying all my breaths then puncturing a breach into layer upon layer of skin.

This is what we humans did: lost in our ephemeral cry for domination, we pillaged and looted relentlessly, replacing life with dead totems, selfish and ambitious beyond all sense of decency. We traded nature for comfort, spontaneity for control, transformation for sameness. Erasing is all we've become, blind to anyone but ourselves. So I welcome you, your thirst a mirror to my own and yet so much more than mere retribution —a defiant howl to experiments and progress. I'll let this feral end consume me and become something new, something I won't see but be part of.

I vaguely sense your roots rummaging my senses, perforating ribs and cavities with living wood. A sun in my darkness, you burn your flaming tourniquet, then press hard and tether, winding your way through my spine, joints and nerves melting as wild green growls within and grey matter bleeds without. I am now an infinite knot of trellises and tendrils, spilling thought morsels onto the soil to fertilize the new spawn of roots, which surely are about to come out.

Unable to collect these morsels into words… I them leave flesh no…

And as this futile human incarnation of mine finally perishes, collapsed into an empty kernel made of vines, a stump appears to be attached still to the root of my decrepit skin—nothing but a bare, useless simulacrum, a weed withered fast. Kudzu knows what to do next. The Earth has taught its roots to tie to life in all its changing forms and be resilient. New crowns instantly sprout, thrusting their way into the rotten hollow of my eye sockets, and racemes start to show, shoots studded with purple inflorescence smelling like grape, fragrant with the deep red blood sucked from human flesh.

Here is how the Earth allows transformation to occur — through rot, renewal and rebirth. Should everything truly end for all of us one day, the world incinerated by our selfish, self-destructive human drive, kudzu will still be here prospering in the last hour of anthropoid greed, leaping into our putrefied pulverized carcasses to become energy, endless and one like the sun swallowing darkness.

(Inspired by Precious Okoyomon's installation "To see the Earth before the end of the world", specifically the section called "Efua, The Sun Is My Own Darkness Swallowed In Flames, An Angel Reborn")

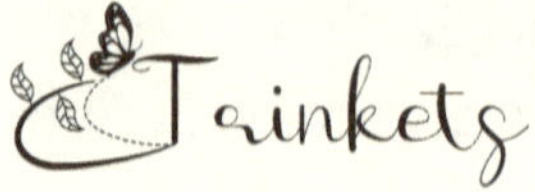

by Margo Pecha

The woman exits her townhome and makes eye contact with me before tossing some peanuts my way. She's done this every morning for the past year. I am grateful, so I bring her gifts from time to time. Little trinkets, shiny things that glint and glimmer in the morning light. The tab from a can of soda. A bit of aluminum foil. She fawns over each and cradles them gently in her hands; humans are so easily pleased.

I flap my wings in acknowledgement and call out to her from my perch on the building across the street, a raucous, guttural caw that carries. She smiles and flutters a little wave in my direction.

She sniffs the air and frowns, noting the same thing I've noticed: Something foul floats through the neighborhood, brought in by the slight breeze. It is rotted and damp and old—there one minute, gone the next. She investigates, purse slung over one shoulder, and pokes her head into the shrubbery, lifts the lids on the garbage cans, cranes her neck down the street. But she cannot find the source of the phantom smell, and so she gets into her car and leaves.

*

A week passes. I find a pebble, smooth and polished with a white band around its middle, and leave it on her doorstep.

She is thrilled, her voice rising in appreciation as she cups it protectively in her hands. I strut proudly along the roofline of the opposing townhomes, watching as she tosses more peanuts onto the stoop before she retreats into the house. Through the window, I see her hand drop the pebble into a jar on the sill, where it nestles among the collection of other gifts I've brought her.

I glide down from the roof and alight on her doorstep. I peck at the nuts, crumbling the shells with my beak and fishing out the tender meats inside, gulping them hungrily. I feel her eyes on me, observing from the window, but I do not mind. This is what we do, she and I.

The smell again, stronger than before, gives me pause. Moldering, decaying, drifting down the street.

I finish the last of the nuts and hop down the steps, turning my head this way and that as I follow the scent. I stop at the curb, peering down into the dark slit of a storm drain. It is strongest here.

There is a wink of eyes in the gloom; a furred figure stares back. I flutter off, startled.

*

Another day, another trinket. I've left her a large button, lustrous and coal-black. She is elated, as always. She scatters the peanuts like confetti, then gets into her car and leaves.

When she returns, her car is laden with paper shopping bags, and the smell in the street is unbearable. She leaves the front door open as she shuttles back and forth, carrying her purchases inside.

It pulls itself from the storm drain when her back is turned, when she's leaning into the trunk—something damp and mildewed and not-quite-humanoid that moves stealthily into her house through the open doorway. I do not know what it is, but I know it is bad from the way that it smells, from the way that it has crept inside. I know it has winking eyes.

I swoop from my perch and slice through the air, diving in front of her as she begins climbing the steps again, arms laden with shopping bags. I flap my wings and make a ruckus, squawking and screeching a warning as I flit about, obstructing her path.

Don't go in! Something bad is in there!

But she doesn't understand. She thinks I want more peanuts. She swats at my beating wings and drops one of the grocery bags. She yells at me and runs inside, slamming the door behind her. I eat the grapes that have rolled from the bag, swallowing them whole.

**

She has not left the house for seven days. The bag of groceries still slumps on the stoop.

I set new offerings on her doorstep—a mossy twig, a lone earring, a small key—but they sit untouched all week. I tap my beak against her window, but the curtains remain drawn. Hunger gnaws deep in my belly, but I am unwilling to abandon the neighborhood. What if she appears while I'm gone?

On the eighth day her door opens and she steps out, disheveled and wobbly. Her stumbling feet scatter the gifts across the steps, and her skin has taken on a sickly pallor, greenish and filmy. The stench of mildew wafts off her as she lurches, unsteady, down the street. She's left the door wide open. I don't think she'll be back.

I drift down to the doorstep and cock my head, peering inside the house—perhaps she keeps the peanuts near the door. The interior yawns, dark and foreboding. I am assaulted by the stench of stagnant water and decay, an undeniable wrongness. I ruffle my feathers and stride away. There is nothing for me here any longer.

I fly off, coasting on unseen currents and turning lazy circles in the air, higher, higher, until the woman is just a speck among specks far below. I keep my eyes trained for something shiny, for peanuts, or for a good perch.

Alison Armstrong

Alison Armstrong is the author of three literary horror novels (*Revenance, Toxicosis,* and *Dark Visitations*), a novella (*Vigil and Other Writings*), in addition to a collection of writings addressing women and horror archetypes (*Consorting with the Shadow: Phantasms and the Dark Side of Female Consciousness).* Having obtained a Master of Arts in English, she has taught composition and literature at Washtenaw Community College in Ann Arbor, MI and Kingsborough Community College in Brooklyn. In addition to her novels and novella (available on Amazon and other online retailers), she has worked as a co-editor of *Nature Triumphs: A Charity Anthology of Dark Speculative Literature* and has had writings published in that anthology, *The Horror Zine Magazine Fall 2025*, as well as several other horror anthologies and *The Sirens Call* ezine. Information on her writings can be found at her Web site: https://horrorvacui.us

Pixie Bruner

Pixie Bruner (HWA/SFPA) is a poet, editor, and cancer survivor. She lives in Atlanta, GA, with her Doppelgänger and pet cats and spiders . Her debut *The Body As Haunte*d (Authortunities Press) was Elgin nominated. Her words are in *Amazing Stories, Strange Horizons, Space & Time Magazine, Hotel Macabre Vol 1* (Crystal Lake Publishing), *Weird Fiction Quarterly,* and more. She wrote for White Wolf Gaming Studio. Werespiders ruining LARPs are her fault. 2025 Kay Snow Award winner and Rhysling Award Chair.

J. Rocky Colavito

J. Rocky Colavito is an ex-college English professor after thirty plus years on the tenure track (and eleven years prior teaching during graduate school). He has relocated to the desert Southwest and is devoting the rest of his days to reading, viewing, and writing horror of all kinds. He is the creator of Buck Neighkyd (porn star turned occult investigator), Vinnie Dark (PI and studio fixer in 1960's Hollywood), the Stoned Cryptid series from Twisted Dreams Press, and writes horror so far ranging that it boggles the mind. Rocky's adventures, ramblings, merch, and books will soon be coming to a conference near you, and, when it's finally finished, at www.plagueprofbooks.net.

Mawr Gorshin

Mawr Gorshin was born Martin Gross in Timmins, Ontario, Canada in 1969. He moved to Taiwan ROC in the summer of 1996, where he's lived ever since, working as a teacher of English as a second language. When not teaching, he has composed music, which has been published on the Jamendo website (classical music under the name 'Martin Gross,' and pop music under the name 'Mawr Gorshin'). He has also written poetry, prose, and analyses of literature, film, and music, as well as articles on narcissistic abuse, all published on his blog, 'Infinite Ocean' (https://mawrgorshin.com/).

https://mawrgorshin.com/
https://www.facebook.com/mawrgorshinwriter/
https://www.facebook.com/mawr.gorshin

Christina Guldi

Christina is a practicing chain-smoking river witch who possesses a deep faith in humanity while simultaneously being chronically disappointed by it. Her favorite style of writing is the revenge letter. Christina has been inspired by her travels and short residences in many places across the United States. She currently resides in Pontiac, Michigan, the poorest city in one of America's richest counties, in order to be surrounded by empty strip malls. She spends time rewilding her lawn and feeding leftover food off customer's plates from whichever restaurant she happens to be working at the time to her neighborhood raccoons and possums. She is proudly not allergic to her cat, Andrew, or poison ivy.

Elad Haber

Elad Haber is a husband, father to an adorable little girl, and IT guy by day, fiction writer by night. He has recent publications from the Simultaneous Times Podcast, Silly Goose Press, Bulb Culture Collective and Does It Have Pockets? His debut short story collection *The World Outside* was published by Underland Press in July 2024. Visit eladhaber.com for links and news.

Kyle Heger

Kyle Heger, former managing editor of *Communication World* magazine, lives in Albany, CA, with his wife and son. His writing has won awards and been accepted by 83 publications, including *London Journal of Fiction, Masticadores Canada* and *Typehouse Literary Magazine.*

Kristi Hendricks

Kristi Hendricks is a poet, fiction writer, and librarian based in Oklahoma. She holds a Master's in Library Studies with a certificate in Archival Studies, and works as a Serials and Electronic Resources Assistant at an academic library. Her writing explores the intersections of nature, sensuality, and transformation. In her ongoing mythos, characters like Andrei and Adrian—half human, half creature of legend—navigate a world where dragons, gryphons, and other ancient forces rise to defend what is wild and sacred. When she isn't writing, Kristi enjoys traveling, birding, and capturing moments of quiet wonder through wildlife photography

Juleigh Howard-Hobson

Juleigh Howard-Hobson's poetry has appeared in *Amazing Stories, The Dead Lands, The Audient Void, Under Her Skin* (Black Spot) *Vastarien: Women's Horro*r (Grimscribe), and many other places. Nominations include the Pushcart, Elgin, Best of the Net and Rhysling. Her latest book is *Curses, Black Spells and Hexes* (Alien Buddha). She is an active member of the HWA, and the 2025 Elgin Award Chair for the SFPA. She lives on the Oregon coast in a suitably haunted 140 year old house.
Bluesky: @juleigh.bsky.social

J. L. Lane

J. L. Lane is a horror author and artist from Cheshire, England. Her debut novella, *Where the Spiders Meet,* launched in 2020—during the apocalypse—followed by its sequel, *When the Spiders Meet,* with the third instalment underway. She also publishes anthologies, offers editing and design services, and runs J. L. Lane Books and J. L. Lane Designs. Lane lives in the Northwest of England with her fiancé, three children, and many pets.

Basile Lebret

While he's French and lives south of Paris, Basile Lebret writes in English. Since it first sprouted in 2022, his work has now spread to over twenty publications in the US, the UK, France or Canada. The most recent include The Horror Zine Spring 2026 Issue, The Alien Buddha Zine 85, God's Cruel Joke, Squirm

Books' Skin Deep and Lowell & Benson's The Dichotomy of Love. Soon in The Anthropocene Epic by Beyond the Star Press. His first collection Welcome to Valenton is being published by Carnage House. Find him on any network: @evoripclaw

LindaAnn LoSchiavo

Native New Yorker LindaAnn LoSchiavo, an award-winning member of British Fantasy Society, HWA, SFPA, and The Dramatists Guild, released three titles in 2024: *Always Haunted: Hallowe'en Poems* (Wild Ink), *Apprenticed to the Night* (UniVerse Press), and *Felones de Se: Poems about Suicide* (Ukiyoto). Next: *Cancer Courts My Mother* (Prolific Pulse Press, 2025) and *Vampire Verses* (Twisted Dreams Press, 2025). Book accolades include the Elgin Award, Chrysalis BREW Project Awards, The World's Best Magazine's Book of Excellence Award, and Spotlyts Story Award. Social media: Blue Sky: @ghostlyverse.bsky.social

Shane David Morin

Shane is an urban poet living in Dover, New Hampshire. His work has been published in Star * Line, Touchstone, and several anthologies, including *Nightmerica: Corruptions of the American Dream, Sleeve of Hearts* and *The Devils Playground: A Horror Charity Anthology for Drug Addiction.* Shane identifies as a feminist and LGBTQIA++ ally and is currently attending the Solstice MFA program at Lasell University. In his spare time, Shane binges Farscape and anything Star Trek.

Irena Barbara Nagler

Irena Barbara Nagler writes and illustrates fiction, poetry, and creative nonfiction. She lives in Michigan, works in libraries, and coordinates a tribe of dancers who embody a weaving of poetry, myth, and the living system of Nature.

Margo Pecha

Margo Pecha lives in southwest Washington state where she writes about obsession, paranoia, and rurality. Her fiction has appeared in *Cosmic Horror Monthly, Fraidy Cat Quarterly,* and various anthologies. When she's not reading or writing, she's working in her gardens and herding chickens.

Sacha Rosel

Sacha Rosel has a summa cum laude four year degree in Foreign Languages and Literatures majoring in English and an MA degree in Oriental Languages and Civilizations. She writes both in English and in Italian. Her work includes lyrical dystopian novella *Pandora, Ricordanza* (Delosdigital, 2024, in Italian); a three-installment (out of five to be published in total) fantastical horror novel set in an imaginary China – installments published so far: *Il libro dei verdi incanti, Il sogno del palazzo scarlatto, La gialla dimora del risveglio* (Delos Digital, 2024-2025, in Italian); experimental novel *Rezia* (Qed, 2025); essay *Una rivoluzione tutta per sé. Cinque scrittrici nella Cina moderna* (Odoya, 2025, in Italian), a feminist literary essay on five Chinese women writers of the modern era (1927-1949) and the mythical horror poem "Awaken to Death" (Memento Mori Ink Magazine, Morsus Vitae magazine, 2025). She has worked as a bookshop assistant, an English-to-Italian fiction translator and as an English teacher. Alongside her website (www.lunadonna.net), mainly in English, she also has her own Substack written in English devoted to reviews and impressions on books and films (http://sacharosel.substack.com/).

Stacy Schonhardt

Stacy Schonhardt is a new author who has been published in two anthologies so far: *Wickedly Able*d (Jan. 2020), and *Scry of Lust 2* (May 2020). Another story will be coming out in the upcoming anthology, *Consumed* (Oct 2025). Stacy has also edited about fifteen books. She lives in the Pacific Northwest with her partner, their puppy, and one oddly long-lived shrimp.

Tamara Kaye Sellman

Tamara Kaye Sellman is co-author of the podcast anthology, Rain Shadows (2025; BTRS Books) and author of Cul de Sac Stories (2024; Aqueduct Press) and Intention Tremor (2021; MoonPath Press). Gnashing Teeth Publishing will release her experimental contemporary fairy tale, Trust Fall, in September 2026. Sellman's speculative fiction is also forthcoming in 2026 (Interesting Times and The Big Book of Quantum Fiction).

Shawn Scott Smith

Shawn Scott Smith is a writer of a bunch of published poems and short stories. He lives in Asheville, NC. He plays pinball and likes to meet new people. All of his adventures are documented on his website at luckycreature.com and most social media spots @luckycreature

David L Tamarin

David L Tamarin is a writer who prefers extreme horror and splatterpunk. He is the author of This Book Hates You 2.0, Hurting My Toys and more. He is also an actor and former entertainment attorney."Mushrooms" was originally published in Gruesome Grotesques Volume 5: The Outer Zone, edited by Trevor Kennedy in 2019.

Tracy Thompson

Tracy L. Thompson is a feminist writing and working in Schenectady, New York. She is a U.S. Navy veteran, and a graduate of the University of South Florida and Yale Law School. She writes poetry, short fiction, memoir, and her debut novel, *Out Like a Lion,* was released in August, 2024. The theme of that work is protecting our freedom from fascism. A member of the Hudson Valley Writers Guild and the Poets of Pyramid Lake, Tracy has also attended the Colgate Writer's conference twice to move her work forward. She is working on her second novel, *Where You'll Find Me,* which she plans to complete in 2026. She has three phenomenal sons, two brilliant grandchildren, and two fur babies who warm her feet as she writes.

www.ingramcontent.com/pod-product-compliance
Lightning Source LLC
LaVergne TN
LVHW051009080826
845145LV00009B/2530

* 9 7 8 1 9 4 5 9 8 7 9 8 4 *